THE OTHER SIDE OF HERE

A Family's Journey

ROSS A. MACINNES

Suite 300 – 990 Fort St
Victoria, BC, V8V 3K2
Canada

www.friesenpress.com

Copyright © 2017 by Ross A. MacInnes
First Edition — 2017

Photography - Front Cover by Linda Finstad
Back Cover by Alexis Schmaltz-Gardiner

All rights reserved.

No part of this publication may be reproduced in any form, or by any means, electronic or mechanical, including photocopying, recording, or any information browsing, storage, or retrieval system, without permission in writing from FriesenPress.

ISBN
978-1-4602-9102-3 (Hardcover)
978-1-4602-9103-0 (Paperback)
978-1-4602-9104-7 (eBook)

1. FICTION
2. FICTION, CHRISTIAN
3. FICTION, FAMILY LIFE

Distributed to the trade by The Ingram Book Company

DEDICATION

I have been blessed throughout my life by the insight, guidance (and sometimes the correction) of wise mentors.

This book is dedicated to the memory of one I value deeply

DR. J.W. GRANT MCEWAN, *OC AOE*
1902 – 2000

CHAPTER ONE

IT WAS MONDAY. AS USUAL, ROOM 406 OF THE FAMILY and Youth Court was packed to capacity. Most teenagers charged with offences were seated with their parents or a social worker on the bare wooden benches laid out in church-like fashion. However, those who had been arrested over the weekend and whose parents had been unable (or unwilling) to make bail were paraded one at a time from a holding room into full view of the court.

A young man stood in the prisoner's dock facing the judge. He was tall for sixteen, almost six feet. A light shadow on his upper lip hinted that an adolescent mustache was just months away. He raised his eyes to meet those of the official.

"This is the second time you have been brought before me," the judge said. "First it was shoplifting, and now possession of drugs. Perhaps the best thing for you would be a six-month term in the juvenile detention hall. You are certainly drawing attention to something going on in your life and, whether you are conscious of it or not, you are asking for someone to put some fences around your actions."

The boy stole a quick glance at his parents, seated in the front row. His father was angry. His tight jaw and clenched teeth betrayed feelings he would have preferred to conceal in dignified surroundings. His mother was afraid. Tears glistened in her eyes and threatened to become a waterfall.

The judge turned his attention to the front row as the mother rose tentatively and remained in a slight crouch. "Yes ma'am—and you are...?" He let the question hang.

"I'm his mother," the woman replied, straightening up a bit. "Is there some way we can get him to settle down and behave without putting him in jail?"

The official looked down at his notes, a pre-sentence report prepared by Probation Services. No indication of any abuse. Parents both professionals. No hints as to why this youngster, with so much going for him, should be headed down a destructive path. He signaled the two parents to approach the raised bench.

He spoke quietly. "Sad to say, many of the young people brought before me don't have their parents with them. As you can see," he raised his eyes and looked over the group assembled, "most of them are with a social worker or a lawyer. I'm pleased that you have chosen to deal with this directly." He looked at his notes again. "There seems to be a lot of potential in this young man, but if things don't change, and change quickly, I will have no choice but to give him a period of incarceration."

Both parents leaned forward as the judge continued in a low voice. "Can you give me any idea as to what's wrong?" he asked, looking from one to the other.

"We're at a loss," the father replied. "It began about a year and a half ago, just when he entered middle school. He started hanging around with new friends, dressing weird, and becoming increasingly separated from us."

"It seems as though he wants to hurt us," the mother added. "Nothing we do has any effect on his behavior." She wiped the corner of her eye with a tissue. "We've tried everything, and nothing seems to get through to him."

The judge took some encouragement from what he was hearing. "Are the two of you committed to keeping this family together?" he asked.

"Yes, we are," the parents replied, almost in unison. After glancing at her husband the mother carried on. "We're willing to do anything. We're afraid he'll get in so deep he'll never be able to get out." The father was nodding.

"He's not too far away from that now," the judge observed. "I've been on the bench for over twenty years, and my experience tells me that determined action must be taken. Things don't get better on their own."

"What do you suggest we do?" the father asked. "We've tried everything—grounding him, taking away privileges, bawling him out, taking him to counselors. Nothing seems to work. I'm really getting frustrated with him!"

The judge did not answer for several moments, then looked intently at the worried parents standing before him. "I'm going to call a brief adjournment in a few minutes. I would like to see the two of you—and your son—in my chambers. The bailiff will escort you."

The parents returned to their seats and Judge Stevenson set the papers aside, motioning to the bailiff that he would be dealing with this particular situation in his chambers. After concluding two other cases he called for a break in the proceedings. The crowd of parents, court workers, lawyers and clients rose as he exited the room.

The elderly bailiff walked down the center aisle immediately after the judge left the room. "Are you the Jamisons?" he asked, as he reached the couple. When they nodded he said, "Would you follow me please?"

Mr. and Mrs. Jamison were escorted through a side exit and down the hallway to an unmarked door. The bailiff knocked lightly and, hearing the invitation to enter, swung it open.

It may have been from watching movies and television, but the Jamisons had expected something quite different from what they saw. There were no deep leather sofas, no mahogany inlaid walls, not even Persian rugs on the floor. There was a small bookshelf against the wall, a commercial-grade desk, and a few government-issue chairs. Seated behind the desk, having removed his black robe, was the judge himself. His guests were surprised to see that underneath the imposing symbol of authority he wore a brightly colored T-shirt.

Seeing the expression on their faces, the judge smiled. "I never did get used to wearing a tie, and my years of dressing up as a practicing lawyer was enough for me. I don't wear one unless I have to. Have a seat," he offered, standing and gesturing toward the chairs. "Your son will join us in a minute."

He had barely finished speaking when they heard a light tapping. "Come," he intoned, moving toward the door. As the young man entered, the judge held out his hand. "Hello Chad," he said, shaking his hand. "Have a seat anywhere. Your mom and dad just got here and I was just telling them how much I hate wearing a tie!"

The informal atmosphere allowed Chad to relax a bit. He had felt tense in the courtroom, prepared for whatever result he faced. Being called to the judge's chambers had thrown his resolve into turmoil, but the casual greeting, the tennis shoes and the T-shirt gave him a feeling that something positive—for once—was about to occur.

The three Jamisons sat facing the judge, now perched on the edge of his desk, one foot touching the floor. "As I mentioned out there," he began, gesturing toward the door, "I am pleased that all of you view this as more than an issue for Chad—as somewhat of a family problem. And both of you," he said, looking at the parents, "have come down to court to see if there's anything that can be done."

"We didn't have much choice," the father responded. "Last night when the police phoned and said Chad had been arrested, they told us to be down here this morning. I'm not sure if we would have come down if they hadn't ordered us."

"But you did come, that's what's important." The judge answered. "I notice also that you didn't go down to the Police Station and bail Chad out last night. May I ask why?"

Chad's mother answered. "We were at our wit's end—still are. We didn't know what to do, so we decided a night in jail might be a good thing." She looked at her son. "We thought maybe if he had a taste of what was in store for him, he'd smarten up and try to avoid trouble."

The judge turned to the young man. "And what about you Chad? Was last night enough to give you an idea what might be ahead for you if you keep on this path?"

Chad shrugged. "I guess."

"See what we have to put up with?" the father remarked, looking from Chad to the judge. "All we get is one-word answers from him." He turned back to Chad. "The Judge asked you a question. Now answer properly!"

The young man slouched down in the chair, legs sprawled and chin on his chest. He mumbled something the adults couldn't hear.

"Speak up Chad!" Mr. Jamison was becoming increasingly frustrated by the actions and attitude of his son, and was in no mood to tolerate Chad's private pity-party.

Chad spoke only slightly louder. "I said 'what does it matter?' You guys are going to decide what you're going to do anyway, so what does it matter what I think?"

"It matters a lot!" The father raised his voice. "It matters because you've screwed up big time! We left you in jail last night to give you something to think about, but obviously it didn't work. Maybe more time is what you need—with an attitude like that!"

The judge allowed the mini-drama to play out. He addressed the three members of the Jamison family. "Do you folks believe in the law?" he asked.

The guests were momentarily stunned by the nature of the question. "Of course we believe in the law," the father answered. Mother and son nodded their agreement.

"I'm not speaking about the laws that are laid down by government; I'm referring to what we call the *laws of the universe*. The laws of man can be broken and man himself can impose certain punishments for those breaches. But laws of nature can't be treated so carelessly." He lifted a ball from off the desk and threw it toward Chad.

Surprised, the young man caught and held it.

"What did you do?" The judge asked.

"I caught it," Chad answered. "Wasn't I supposed to?"

"That was up to you. What would have happened to the ball if you hadn't caught it?"

"I guess it would have kept going and hit the wall. Throw it again and I won't stop it," Chad said, a challenge in his voice.

The judge continued, unperturbed by Chad's remark. "What you did was prove Newton's first law of motion: *an object in motion tends to stay in motion unless acted upon by an outside force.* That is, objects tend to keep on doing what they're doing until something intervenes. I threw the ball. It would have kept moving, but you stopped it. You see Chad, I'm a judge. I not only have to look at what happened and impose some sort of consequence, but I also have to consider what will keep it from happening again. I could impose a jail sentence—and maybe I will have to—but I'm not convinced even that would be enough to cause a permanent change in your pattern of behavior. What I *do* believe is that left unchecked, your actions will continue in the same manner and may result in something tragic. Like the ball, you would hit the wall."

The parents looked at each other in confusion. What was he talking about? "I'm sorry Judge, I'm not sure I understand what you're getting at," Mr. Jamison protested. "What has Newton's law got to do with Chad?"

"Simply this. Chad, and indeed this family, is moving in a certain direction. Unless something is done to change that direction, things will continue as they are. My task is to apply or assign an outside force sufficient to change the path." He turned to Chad. "I've read the accounts of what happened, and I've read the pre-sentence report." His voice was stern. "I am not going to let this continue. Your life is chaotic at the moment and will continue that way unless something happens. I intend for something to happen."

Judge Stevenson looked at the father and paused, struggling with the decision he was about to make. Then the corners of his mouth softened a little. "I'm going to release the young man into your custody," he said. "You both seem committed to your son, but it's going to take more than that—a lot of work—on everyone's part. And if you are truly dedicated to rebuilding this family, I think there may be a way." He took a piece of paper from the desk drawer, and began drawing a map.

When he was finished he handed the sheet of paper to the young man's father. "I am directing you to go, as a family, to spend some time at this place. I'm not establishing any minimum or maximum time limits—that will be up to you and the hosts of the place—nor am I going to place conditions on what you do or not do once you're there. All I'm asking for is your effort. Is that acceptable?"

The pair nodded in agreement.

The judge then turned to the boy. "Young man. I'm letting you go home with your parents. I'm not looking for your approval or agreement. It's been my experience that when a teenager's life is in chaos, promises are easily made, and just as easily broken. So, I'm not seeking any promises. But I will say, that time is running out for you." He stood, signaling the private conference was about to end.

Upon being paged, the bailiff returned to the judge's chambers and escorted the family through the hallway to the public area in the front of the building.

"I hope you've learned your lesson" the father said as soon as the bailiff had left. "This is humiliating for both your mother and I. You have no idea what you're putting us through. How can you be so selfish?"

"We're very worried," his mother added. "We've tried so hard to give you everything. We don't know where we went wrong. And now the judge says this is your last chance. Next time he'll put you in jail. Can you understand at all how scared we are?"

The young man looked up. "How come it's always about you guys? You say you're scared. What about me? Don't I have something to say in all this?"

"No you don't!" his father exploded. "Weren't you listening? The judge said he wasn't looking for your agreement or promises or anything from you other than to straighten up and quit being so stupid!"

The woman put her hand on her husband's arm. "Let's go somewhere we can talk. People are staring."

Looking at his son in disgust, the father turned and walked ahead of his wife and son to an isolated spot away from the crowded area in front of the building.

"What do you think?" the woman asked her husband. "Is this guy serious? Can we trust him. I know he's a judge and all, but what if he's with some cult or something?"

"I don't think he's with a cult," came the reply, "but I am concerned that he might be some kind of religious fruitcake on a crusade to save the world."

They were startled when the Judge appeared at their side. "I'm sorry I can't give you more detailed information," he said, stopping and facing them. "You've sent your son to counselors, psychiatrists, probation officers—even a couple of well-meaning friends. Is that right?"

The parents nodded, still uncertain of the judge's intentions.

"It's not that they don't work. It's just that sometimes a family can't seem to come together on things. It isn't just one person who needs help—it's the whole family. While your son may be the one who has come before the courts, it involves all of you." He looked at the three of them. "It's not a son problem, it's a family problem."

The father opened his mouth to object, but the judge held up his hand. "I know that what I'm saying hurts a bit, but isn't this thing impacting your whole family?"

"I'm not sure what you mean." The father finally got a word in.

"Do you normally take a day off from work and hang around the courthouse?" He looked at Mrs. Jamison. "Or you? Is it typical for you to spend half an hour in a judge's office?" Both shook their heads. "And Chad. Isn't there something else you'd rather be doing with your mom and dad than listening to some guy in running shoes and a black dress?"

They laughed nervously. Then the father became serious again. "Okay, we've tried everything else, it seems, what do we do in your program?"

"It's not my program—it's yours," the judge replied. "If you're willing to make a commitment to work together, and stick with it to the end, I assure you'll come through this experience with not only a united family but also a deeper understanding of yourselves."

"Well, I must say we're intrigued." The father seemed to be relaxing a bit. "It's not how we usually do things, but we're willing to commit to whatever we need to do. What's next?"

"Follow the directions I gave you. You have a few things to arrange this afternoon, such as dealing with time off from your jobs and contacting your son's school, but you should try to be up there by suppertime. It's a three-hour drive—I hope you can read my map."

CHAPTER TWO

SCATTERED CLOUDS ABOVE THE LAKE DRIFTED OFF IN the early afternoon, chased by a gentle breeze that eased them westward and over the horizon. A bald eagle, wings catching the upper edge of a draft, soared over an old hunting lodge on the crest of a hill overlooking the water.

Behind the lodge, partially hidden by dense fir trees, stood a small barn. Milling quietly, four Appaloosa horses nibbled grass shoots growing near the corral posts. Spotted patches on their rumps reflected the rays of the afternoon sun.

To the north of the lodge, the outline of a roadway was barely visible through the branches of the birch and aspen trees. A couple of hundred yards from the front steps, the road curved through a clearing, dipped through the creek bed and continued winding toward the main thoroughfare.

Emerging from the trees, a slow-moving figure made his way down a path leading to the front porch. He ambled along, enjoying the late-summer rays that filtered through the leaves and laid a dappled pattern on the dusty surface. He was an older man, probably in his mid-seventies, taking his time and soaking up nature's sensations as he walked along. He heard the whisper of the breeze through the trees, the cry of the eagle circling high overhead, and the sound of lake water lapping on the shore below the lodge. As the warmth of the sun filtered through the foliage touched his face, he paused a moment to watch a squirrel scamper up a nearby tree.

He was a quiet man, content with what life had handed him, and took joy in the tasks he had been given. As he started up the narrow footpath to the front porch, his presence seemed to complete a scene of perfect peace and contentment.

He paused on the stairs and turned to look out over the lake. "You always give such nice gifts," he said, "and I know I don't thank you as often as I should." He settled himself on the porch swing, his gaze traveling across the quiet water to the far shore. "Just look at the hills over there—quite a sight, as you know. Trees are still green, but in a week or two—maybe a month at most—they'll be turning red and gold and all sorts of colors."

"Who are you talking to, Charlie?" The voice came from inside.

"Oh, just God and I having a little chat" he responded. "I know He can see the hills and trees and the water, but once in a while I just want to bring His attention back to Lake Sandoza. In case He gets distracted with all the other stuff going on and forgets there is still some beauty left in this old world."

"Well, I'm sure we forget about Him more often than He forgets about us," the woman said as she opened the door behind him. She carried a glass of cold lemonade in her right hand and offered it to him. "Did you have a good trip to town?"

"Thanks, dear. The trip was good", he replied. "In fact I picked up a message from Judge Stevenson. He's sending another family up here. Should be arriving today just in time for supper." He took a long sip of the tangy beverage. "Ah, just what I needed—that was a long walk, but a good one."

"Did you remember to put up the sign at the corner? We don't want our guests to get lost driving up here."

Charlie nodded. "Yes I did. Now, if the Judge remembered to note on the map where the corner is, and for the new folks to take down the sign after they turn, we should be okay. He's never missed yet, but these youngsters have a bit of a brain freeze now and then."

"And how is Ray?" she asked. "I was so pleased when he was appointed Family and Youth Court Judge. Can't say I'm surprised though. I always thought he'd make something of himself one day."

Charlie smiled. "Bess, you think every youngster who comes up here is going to change the world. I'm not blaming you for believing, but some are going to be very content taking a lower profile and just doing their best, you know? We just have to give our best with the families that come our way."

"I know," she said settling down beside him on the swing. "But I get so excited when they're around, and since the Connors left, it's been a bit empty around here. I'm anxious to see who Ray, er... Judge Stevenson, has for us this time."

"You know; I was thinking on the way back from town just how honored we are to be in this place at this time. To have families entrusted to our care is such a privilege. And then to have the parents place their child in our care, and to believe that those new lives can be changed, just leaves me speechless!"

Bess slipped her arm around Charlie's shoulder and gave him a hug. "You're right. We couldn't have dreamed thirty-some-odd years ago that we'd be doing this, could we?"

Charlie rested his cheek on Bess's head. "No, we sure couldn't have. Do you remember the first time we came up that old road? It was winter wasn't it?"

"No, you old goof, you know it wasn't! I don't know why you keep thinking it was winter. It was late spring. Oh, there might have been some snow left under the trees, but don't you remember we had to leave the car down the road a bit because there was water in the creek?"

"Oh yes, now I remember. I also remember how I had to carry you over that little trickle of water because you didn't want to get your new shoes wet!

"We must have been a sight. Two city slickers coming up to the bush for a weekend getaway—we had no idea what was in store for us did we?"

"No, we sure didn't." Charlie put his hands in the small of his back and stretched. "But it's been a wonderful thirty years."

They sat in cozy companionship, sharing memories of their years at the century-old lodge. They had come up to Lake Sandoza at a critical time in their lives. Both had been involved in hectic careers, and their marriage was, at best, a convenient living arrangement.

"Do you ever wonder what would have become of us if we hadn't taken the time to drive up here or met Daniel and Mary?" Bess mused.

"Yes, occasionally, but I do believe there was a force at work that would have eventually brought us here regardless of our stubbornness." Charlie lapsed into silence.

After a few moments, Bess stood, picking up the empty glass. "Well, I guess I better get ready for the new arrivals. Do we know anything about them? Did Ray leave any information at all?"

"Now, you know better than that." Charlie chuckled. "The rules are that they don't know anything about us—or the lake—and we don't know anything about them. That's what makes this so great. No prejudging anything. We just work together to help, hoping that each family that comes up here takes something special with them when they leave. But they all pass on something wonderful to us as well."

The porch floor creaked as Bess walked over and leaned against the railing, arms straight, head up, as she had done countless times. "Just smell the scent of pine coming in off the lake!" She inhaled the afternoon breeze. "It's something I can never get over—how fresh and quiet it is."

"I think I smell something else that I can never get too much of," her husband joked. "Is that apple pie?"

"Never you mind" she scolded, smiling. "That's for supper. And with the new family arriving at any minute, you'll have to limit yourself to one piece."

"Oh, I know, I know. But have you ever considered that maybe one of these days one of the families that come up here won't like apple pie? Have you ever considered that?"

Bess turned and looked lovingly at her husband. "No, I've never considered that, but obviously you have. Now, before they arrive, why don't you head up to the barn and see if Pete and Janet can come down for supper and meet the new arrivals?"

"You mean Pete and Repeat," Charlie chuckled, referring to the way they always worked together around the horses—and with the young people who came up to the lake. Charlie stood and stretched. Giving Bess a quick kiss on her upturned cheek, he stepped off the porch and started up the trail to the barn.

The pathway, lined with rocks on either side, wound through a grove of trees. Each rock had been lovingly placed by a previous guest, and remained a symbol of the enduring values imparted here.

Approaching the corral attached to the barn, Charlie put his fingers to his mouth and gave a quick whistle. Around the corner came a big collie, wagging his tail and stretching as he ambled over to the man.

"Hiya Smudge" Charlie said, stooping down to give him a quick scratch behind the ear. "Where's your master?"

"That's a bit sexist, don't you think?" came a response from inside the barn. A dark-haired woman in her early thirties emerged from within the shadows, slapping the dust off her jeans. "You men assume a whole lot because a dog is called man's best friend—ain't so around here. I'm Smudge's best friend! Ain't I Smudge?"

The big collie wagged his tail in agreement and abandoned the ear scratching in favor of attention from the woman.

"I stand corrected. As I can see, he much prefers your company to mine. What I really came up here for is to invite you and Pete down to the house for supper. We're expecting a new family anytime now, and Bess wondered if you'd like to join us?"

"It's about time we had some new guests. Pete and I were just talking about that, and wondered when we would be heading out on the trail again. Any idea who they are?"

"You know the judge. He never gives any information about the families he sends up here. We all agreed there was a great danger in jumping to conclusions about people by having negative information about them, but it would be nice once in a while to at least know the gender of the kids coming up, or how many there are. Could be a bunch or just a few." Charlie placed his right foot on the bottom rail of the fence. "But since we all agreed to the conditions, I guess we'll have to abide by them."

Janet came over to stand beside him, linking her arm in his, like a daughter about to chide her father. "If you think it's tough for us not having any information, can you imagine what it's like for the folks coming up? All they get is a map and a list of things to bring."

"They have to have a lot of faith to do that—faith and hope. Hope that things work out—that the family can heal and the kids get back on track." He stepped back and looked into Janet's eyes. "You know some folks say they wish their child was better behaved, or they wish their marriage was stronger—they wish for this or that. What they don't realize is the great difference between *wishes* and *hopes*."

Although Janet had listened to Charlie wax eloquent on this topic more than once, she leaned back against the rails, hooked the heel of her boot over the bottom bar as he had done, and let him continue.

The pair turned as a tall man in denims, a checkered shirt and battered Stetson, came out of the barn and joined them. "What're you guys gabbing about?" he asked.

"Oh, Charlie's getting philosophical about the subtle difference between wishes and hopes. And...he's invited us down for supper. Seems a new crew's arriving this afternoon."

Pete moved into the sunshine. "Well, speaking of hope, I sure hope Bess has a harvester-size meal on the stove. I haven't eaten all afternoon. Shiloh, the new gelding, threw a shoe yesterday when we were up on the ridge above the camp, and I've spent most of the day putting on a new one."

"I'm sure Bess has plenty of food," Charlie replied. "She has this uncanny knack for knowing when folks are coming. Can we expect you for supper then?"

"Sure, we'd love to come down. We have a couple of things to do and after we wash up, we'll be ready."

Charlie nodded, smiled, and started back to the Lodge. As he walked he reflected on the families that had come to the place and experienced changes in their lives—subtle changes for some, profound for others. The common thread was that all of them had experienced a change of heart.

He recalled the Thatcher's—a family torn apart by a bitter divorce. Two teenage girls feeling unwanted and unloved, caused by the constant rancor between their parents. *Why can't adults understand that children are a part of each of them? And when one parent ridicules or disparages the other, the child can't help but feel the disrespect. Children are also part of the absent parent.* Charlie remembered how difficult it was for the Thatcher's to understand this, and to change their feelings and actions toward one another. But they did. They didn't get back together, but they did learn to respect and value their ex-partner's way of life and to work together in the best interests of their daughters.

Or the MacDonald family. What a group that was! Seven in all—two boys and three girls—ranging from seven to nineteen. At first, bringing the family together looked to be impossible. From drug abuse to runaways, it appeared that it was just a matter of a short few days before the family would totally fall apart.

Charlie had developed a friendship with a nearby rancher who specialized in working with rescue horses, and had developed a program using the horses in a therapeutic setting. Charlie had decided to give him a call.

Persuading the MacDonald parents to consider spending a weekend at the Triple R Ranch was not difficult. They had almost given up and were willing to try anything. Even *that horse stuff* as they called it.

The results were amazing.

Maybe some time with the horses is what this family needs, Charlie thought.

Charlie stopped when he heard the familiar sound of water. A rivulet flowed from a spring higher up the hill and passed under the path. He always paused to draw strength from the babbling water. Now he knelt to rearrange a couple of stones to alter the flow and create a new sound.

As he bent down he noticed, in the soft soil at the edge of the water, the footprints of a raccoon. He could see where the animal had stood on its hind legs, and where it had cracked the shell of a hazelnut and eaten the soft meat inside, leaving a small pile of debris. He marveled at the instinct that enabled the raccoon to use his front feet as hands to wash the nut, then peel away the hard shell with his front teeth to obtain the kernel inside. He had heard or read somewhere that a raccoon didn't actually wash its food before eating, it merely used the water to help swallow and digest its food. Charlie stood, still gazing at the tracks and trying to fathom nature's miracles.

Suddenly he remembered the new arrivals. He was anxious to meet them, and hoped they would find the peace that other families had found. Would this be the family he and Bess and been waiting for?

CHAPTER THREE

THE RAMBLING TWO-STORY CAME INTO VIEW AS Charlie emerged from the trees. He had just put his foot on the step when he heard the sound of a car approaching. Looking down the roadway he could make out the hood of a vehicle as it stopped at the creek. He watched to see the reaction of the driver. On more than one occasion a family had turned back, using the barrier of the small gully as an excuse. He hoped that this family—whoever they were—had the determination to follow through on the hope generated by Judge Stevenson.

The large sedan eased its way down the far bank and the front wheels touched the water. Charlie clapped his hands. Yes! Now they were committed. As the vehicle wound its way closer, Charlie called to his wife. "Bess, they're here!"

The door opened behind him, and the matron of the house came and stood alongside. Both were excited about the new arrivals. It was always a thrilling time for the group at the lake when new guests came to stay. There was a sense of expectancy and, although no one ever admitted it, a tinge of apprehension that, this time, the task would prove too much for them.

They moved back onto the porch when the car stopped beside the steps. Silence descended once again when the driver turned the ignition off and the motor died. The driver's door swung open and a man got out. "I'm not sure if we have the right place," he said as he walked around the front of the car. "We're the Jamison's. Are you expecting us?"

The two older folks descended the steps as Charlie said, "We're expecting a family, and if you were given a map by Judge Stevenson, then you have the right place."

The younger man nodded. "Well, we have the map, but know nothing at all about why we're up here."

"I'm Miriam Jamison", a woman said as the front passenger door swung open, "and if you're thinking of selling us land or a condominium, you can forget it. We're only here because we were ordered to come. If I had my way, I'd report that so-called judge to the authorities."

Bess chortled as she walked over to the younger woman. "No, we're not selling land or time-shares. I'm Bess and this is my husband, Charlie. And we're as in-the-dark as you folks. Oh, we can guess why you're here, but we don't have any information about who you are or why you've been asked to come."

Charlie walked over and shook hands with the man. "And you're...?" he asked.

"I'm Ian Jamison", the man replied holding out his hand. "We weren't even told how long we'd be staying—just to pack enough outdoor clothing for a week or two and if we stayed longer we could wash them. I had a bit of problem explaining this to my boss, but I did get some time off, and Miriam was able to book some vacation time. Chad was no problem as he had already been suspended from school so, we're here for Chad's big adventure." There was an undercurrent of cynicism as he spoke the name of his son.

"It's an adventure for all of us," Charlie responded as he shook hands with Miriam. "And I would assume you are Chad" he added, stooping to speak into the open window of the car's back seat.

"Ya, I'm Chad—the *bad son* as my parents will tell you." The door swung open and a young man got out. He was mid-teens, and built like his father. He also had the same hair and eye color as his dad.

"Well, come into the house." Charlie spoke to all three of them. "Can I help you with your bags?"

"Thanks, but we only brought enough for the week, so there's only the three." Ian replied as he popped the trunk open, lifted the cases out and set them on the ground. "Chad, can you carry your mother's case up to the house? And put mine on the step. I'll and move the car out of the way."

"Why can't she take it herself? I don't even want to be here—staying with some old geezers up on Walton's Mountain!" The young man's voice rose as he grabbed his bag and headed for the house.

"Just a second there," Ian said sharply. He strode over to his son, grabbed him by the shoulder and spun him around. "The only reason we're up here is because of you. Or would you rather be in kiddy jail? Because that's where you're going if you keep up that attitude!"

"Oh, Ian, just let him be for a while okay?" the mother intervened. "He's tired from the long trip. I'm sure he's looking forward to being here, aren't you Chad?"

"Yes, Mom, I'm ecstatic," the teenager snarled. "Just look around will you? No stores, no people, no nothing. I bet they don't even have electricity. I'm just jumping for joy; can't you tell?"

"We do have electricity," Bess said to Chad. "But we don't have television and we don't have a phone. And, we're even out of cell-phone range. I know it'll take some getting used to, but we do have some interesting things going on around here, as you'll find out in the days to come. Just give it a chance, okay?"

"Whatever," Chad replied.

Ian turned to Charlie. "That's his response to everything—*whatever*! Or if we ask him a question about something, his response is *nothing*. Sorry you folks had to see this as soon as we got here, but I sure hope you can fix this kid so he changes his attitude."

Charlie ignored the implied question and motioned toward the house. "Let's get your things into the house and have some supper. You folks haven't eaten, have you?"

"Well, we did stop for a burger a couple of hours ago. We weren't sure what was going on so we decided the best thing was to grab a bite when we could. Oh, I almost forgot. The note the judge gave us said that after we turned off the main road we were to take down the sign for the place and bring it to you." He dug in the trunk of the car and brought out the sign indicating the name of the Lodge. "Here it is."

"Thanks, I'll put it over here". Charlie carried the sign over and leaned it against the porch. "Come on, we'll show you your rooms. We'll have supper in about half an hour, and a young couple will be joining us at the table." Bess opened the screen door and invited the group inside.

Miriam was the first to enter, and as she crossed the threshold to the huge living room she stopped abruptly. Chad, carrying his bag and fiddling with his cell-phone in an attempt to get reception, bumped into her. "That's, that's—"Miriam stuttered, pointing to a photo on the wall.

"Yup, may be a face or two you'll recognize." Charlie said, standing beside her. "As you can see, we have a lot of photos. Some old, some newer, but every one of them, at one time or another, have been guests here at the lake." Having briefly clarified the reason for the photos, Charlie guided the group toward the stairway that led to the upper floor.

After being shown their rooms, the Jamisons unpacked and prepared for supper. Before going downstairs again, Ian said to his wife. "Just what kind of place is this? We have to do what the judge ordered, but I have some serious concerns. I was kind of expecting a more formal place, at least some staff with some experience and training dealing with problem teenagers. I don't know if they'll get Chad to be civil, let alone come to grips with his problems."

Miriam turned from folding the clothes into the chest of drawers. "I certainly didn't like the way Chad was acting in front of these folks—if he didn't like things he should have waited until they were out of earshot. But I don't blame him for being concerned about this place.

After all, they admitted they didn't have TV, so I can see a very boring week for him. And you know what he's like if he gets bored!"

"Well, we'll just see how things go for tonight. If it's going to be as laid back and disorganized as they appear right now, we'll just pack our stuff and head back to town. We've done what the Judge asked—we're up here—and it's not our fault if these folks can't help Chad. At least we tried." Putting on a brave face, they went downstairs.

Bess was placing the last bowl of hot food onto the table. "Just grab a chair and pull up to the table. Pete and Janet are just out on the porch with Charlie, so we're ready to sit down as soon as Chad comes down."

The screen door thumped, and Charlie, with Pete and Janet, both in blue jeans, made their way to the table.

"Ian and Miriam, I'd like to introduce Janet and Pete." The couple shook hands warmly with the Jamisons. "Pete and Janet are our wranglers, and do all the guiding on the trail rides up here," Charlie continued as he gestured for everyone to take their places at the table. "They'll be spending a lot of time with Chad during your stay."

As if cued by an unseen stagehand, Chad entered. "What's this about me?" he inquired, pulling out a chair and slumping into it.

Pete turned and looked at Chad. "Janet and I will be spending some time with you over the next little while—if that's alright with you? We'd like to take the horses and head up into the hills—give you a look at some pretty incredible country."

"No thanks. I don't like horses, I don't like being around them and I don't like riding them. Besides, the order was for us to come up here. The judge didn't say anything about having to go on a horseback ride." Turning to his parents he said, "How long are we going to stay? I have some stuff I need to do back home."

"Chad, please," Miriam pleaded. "We just got here. We haven't even had a chance to talk. We'll stay the night and discuss it tomorrow." She smoothed her hair nervously as she glanced around the table.

"Fine! Don't discuss anything with me. As if I ever get to make any decisions."

Ian's face flushed. He was embarrassed by his son's outburst. "Chad. We talked in the car on the way up here, and you promised you would give whatever was asked a fair try. So that'll be enough for now and, as your mother said, we'll discuss it tomorrow."

The teen lowered his eyes and sulked in silence.

Conversation around the table was tentative, as the adults talked about the weather and other trivial matters.

After supper Charlie began gathering the dishes and taking them to the kitchen sink. He was joined first by Pete and then by Ian. "When Bess cooks, I wash up, and when I cook—and I'm a fair hand in the kitchen I might add—then Bess does the tidying up."

Charlie washed and the other men dried, while the three women remained at the table. After finishing his meal, Chad had left quickly, saying he was going outside for a cigarette.

The afternoon sun, which had provided a magnificent day, settled leisurely behind the distant snowcaps. As dusk descended over the lodge Charlie placed a couple of pine logs on the hearth of the immense stone fireplace. Its chimney rose a full sixteen feet to a post-and-beam ceiling and the huge wooden mantle supported an eclectic mix of pictures, handcrafted mementoes, and an old lantern. Propped against the rear of the ledge was the rusted remnant of an old rooftop weathervane with a crowing rooster in front.

Scattered randomly throughout the room were large easy chairs. Each one had been crafted from various logs taken from the property. Charlie began dragging one of the chairs over toward the front of the fire, and Ian joined him, helping to bring other seats to the hearthside. Pete pointed to the door, signaling he was heading outside. "I'll just join Chad on the porch if you don't mind," he said. "I'd like to explain what I meant by going for a ride in the hills."

"And I think I'll go on up to the stables." Janet said, as Pete was leaving. "If we're heading out tomorrow, I'd like to bring the horses into the barn and give them a bit of oats—their comfort food." She smiled and thanked Bess for supper, then briefly joined Pete and Chad on the porch before walking up to the barn.

Bess and Miriam joined Charlie and Ian in the overstuffed chairs in front of the fire. The men loosened their belts and praised the feast that Bess had prepared, with particular compliments on the apple pie.

"This is the most comfortable I've felt in ages," Ian said, slipping out of his brogues and resting his feet on a log close to the fire. "I usually watch television after supper, but this is a nice change."

"I'm so pleased you enjoyed the meal, and thank you for the compliment," Bess said, pushed her chair back from the fire and standing up. "I'm going to put on some coffee and tea. What would everyone like?"

"I'd like some coffee, please", Ian replied. "However I'm still not clear on what's going on. I think you folks are great, and this is a terrific place, but I must say I have some concerns." He picked up the poker from fireplace and jabbed at a burning log. "Look at it from our point of view. This morning we were in court. Then out of the blue, we rearranged our lives, took time off from work, drove three hours following a hand-scribbled map, to meet people we never heard of. And now we're told our son's going on some trail ride with strangers. And we have no idea what we—Miriam and I—are supposed to do or how long we're supposed to stay. I think we deserve an explanation."

CHAPTER FOUR

CHAD WAS LEANING ON THE RAILING WHEN PETE opened the door and walked onto the porch. He was carrying an empty coffee can and set it on the floor beside the teen. "For your butts. It's dry up here this time of year so we have to take a few extra precautions." He stood beside the young man and looked out over the yard and lake.

The tip glowed brightly as the teen took a final drag on his cigarette, then dropped it into the can. "Are you out here to bug me about smoking?"

"Well, what I think is less important than what you think," Pete replied. "I used to smoke so I know that there are some personal reasons for doing so. I found it a very expensive habit, and I could never get my teeth white." He smiled, taking care what he said and how he said it. "But ultimately, Chad, what we do is up to us as individuals. We can choose to smoke—or not. We can choose to go to school—or not. We can choose who to date, who to associate with, what we wear. Ultimately we are responsible for what we do and how we do it."

"That's crap!" the young man exploded. "I didn't choose to come up here—the judge ordered me to. I didn't choose to go to school, that's the law. There's lots of things I have to do that I don't want to. If I had my choice, I'd be on my own in my own apartment with my own friends and doing the things I want—not what my parents or some judge wants."

Pete didn't say anything for several minutes. Finally, he turned and looked directly at Chad. "About fifteen years ago I had a conversation very similar to the one we're having now. Except that I was the teenager and Charlie was the one who was leaning against this railing trying to get inside my head. I was as ticked off about his interfering in my life as you are right now. I didn't want to listen, but he said something that made me stop and think just long enough to hear what he was actually saying. He asked me *is there anything about your life right now that you would like to change?* I had to answer yes."

"But, I was still hooked on the idea that if only I had decent parents, things would be okay. Or, if only I could get a job. If only I could do this, or do that, then everything would be okay." Pete pointed to the steps. "Let's sit down for a minute, all right?"

They sat on the porch, feet on the steps, elbows on knees. Pete looked across the yard toward the lake. "You see, I thought that if other people would change, or if some circumstance would change, then I could get on with my life and everything would work out the way I wanted. So I'll ask you the same question Charlie asked me. Is there something in your life you want to change?"

"Of course I want something to change—I already told you. I want to get my own apartment and do the things I want." Chad replied angrily. "But I won't be able to do that with this court order forcing me to come up here."

"I agree. The reality is the court order and you being here. That's a given. When Charlie talked with me way back when, he took the time to show me that there is such a thing as reality. No, I didn't have a court order, but I didn't want to be here, and the change I wanted to happen would require that other people change—not me. And that's human nature—wanting other people to change. But over time I learned that all I could control was my thoughts, beliefs, attitudes and actions—no one else's."

The young man remained silent, but he was listening.

"So Charlie asked me if I wanted to change anything I had control over. That was difficult for me. I was so used to blaming others and believing that things were out of my control and that nothing would change for me unless others did some serious readjusting of their lives."

"You're saying I should give up smoking, is that it?" Chad shook another cigarette from the pack and lit it. "That's about the only thing I have control over."

"Let's go for a walk". Without waiting for Chad's reply, Pete stood and descended the steps. He stopped briefly at the bottom of the stairs and glanced back at the teen.

Reluctantly the young man stood, tossed his smoke into the tin and joined Pete. "Where are we going?"

"No place in particular. I just find that sometimes I can think better when I'm walking." He started moving slowly. "You asked if I was saying you should give up smoking. As I said earlier, that's your decision and what I think, say or do about it is of less importance than what you think or do about it. What I did say was that you are the only person who can make a choice about yourself. Other people may offer their opinions about your actions, make decisions that greatly affect you, or even establish controls over what you do. But you have a choice about whether to accept those opinions, decisions or controls. Do you understand what I'm saying?"

"Maybe. What you're telling me is that my parents or the courts or teacher or someone else can tell me to do something or not do something, but I have a choice in whether I do it or not. I don't see how I have any choice in any of that stuff."

They walked along the dusty lane to where the vehicles were parked. "Let me try it from another angle," Pete said as he lowered the tailgate on his old pickup and sat on the edge. "When I was younger, I arrived up here because I was sleeping on the streets and stealing to survive—at least that's how I excused it. I knew that stealing was wrong. I had been told by my dad, and I knew deep inside me that taking something from someone without their permission was dishonest. I also knew there would be punishment if I got caught. I knew that I shouldn't do it, but I made a choice—in spite of all those controls—to do it anyway. You see, ultimately, it was my choice."

Waving his hand at the surrounding area, Chad held on to his stubbornness like a kid hanging on to a tinker toy. "Are you telling me that I chose to be up here? If you think that, you're crazy! Like I said, I'm only up here because that idiot judge ordered us up here. I didn't have any choice in the matter!"

"I know I'm ticking you off Chad, but let me pose a question to you. You don't have to answer it if you don't want to, but maybe it's something to consider. The actions that brought you to the attention of the courts, was it something that you knew was wrong to do?"

"I don't think it's wrong—maybe other people do. I mean...didn't you smoke a joint sometimes when you were my age?"

"Actually Chad, I did. But let's think a bit more about smoking the joint. Had you been told by anyone that it was wrong?"

"Yeah, I watched a film at school and my dad told me he would punish me big time if I ever did drugs."

"But you did anyway, right?"

"Yeah, so what?"

"Well, didn't you make a conscious choice not to obey your father? And, in spite of the warnings at school, didn't you decide for yourself to try some weed?"

Chad looked at Pete, teeth clenched. "Okay, so if that's what you're driving at, yes, I did choose to do a joint, and yes, in spite of my father or anyone else. I didn't think it wrong then, and I don't now. So what's your point?"

Pete slid down off the tailgate and walked to the drivers' side of the truck. "My point is this Chad. We all have choices we have to make. Even avoiding making a decision is a choice. We can defy rules and regulations, or just not follow them. We can disobey an order or just ignore it. Whatever we do, we are making a decision, a choice."

Slipping behind the steering wheel, Pete put the key in the ignition, and started the truck. "I assume you have a driver's license?" he asked, revving the motor, then getting out of the truck.

Chad seemed puzzled by the abrupt change in Pete's approach. "Yeah, I have a license, so what?"

Pete began to walk back toward the Lodge, then turned and stopped. "Chad, you have a choice to make. I want you to be a part of what's happening here, and head up to the mountains tomorrow with Janet and me. You don't want to be here, but you feel you have no choice. I'm telling you that you've always had a choice, and you do now. I'm going to leave you with the truck. You can take it back to the city—it's full of gas—and I'll tell the judge this place is not going to work for you and he will accept my report and impose no further punishment. I will also tell your folks that you were given this option and that I take full responsibility. It's now in your hands, Chad. It's your choice."

Chad stood open-mouthed, looking first at the truck and then at the retreating figure of a man named Pete, who was playing the game by different rules. He raised his middle finger in defiance, kicked the side of the box. Then he opened the door of the idling vehicle.

CHAPTER FIVE

AS JANET LEFT THE GROUP TO HEAD UP TO THE horses, Charlie stood to help his wife pour coffee for Ian and Miriam. "I don't blame you for feeling troubled about what's taking place, and I agree you deserve some explanation of what's happening.

"You see, this old lodge is a special place, and has, over the years, seen many folk sit around this fire and begin, sometimes for the first time, to come to grips with what is occurring in their families. It isn't a resort or vacation destination, although most find that they leave here refreshed in body, mind and spirit. Nor is it a religious organization, although a heart once opened to the spiritual wonder of nature can never again be fully closed. It is not part of any government program or national group. It does not advertise, promote or open itself to bookings or reservations. It exists for only one reason—the rebuilding of families that are experiencing life-altering struggles."

Charlie set his mug on the edge of the hearth and gave it a quick stir with the spoon. He adjusted his chair so he could look directly at Miriam and Ian, and then settled back into the padded fabric. "The influenza outbreak in 1893 caused incredible suffering and many fatalities throughout the nation, particularly in the cities. One couple in their early forties lost four children to the epidemic. The woman was the daughter of a wealthy industrialist and her husband was a physician. The loss of their children almost destroyed them, and what was so very difficult to handle was that, in spite of their wealth and medical skills, they were unable to prevent the tragedy in their family."

All eyes were on Charlie as he related how this couple became resolute in their mission to provide a place of respite to other families who had undergone heartbreak and tragedy, and required a time of healing to refresh, restore and rebuild their lives.

When the fire had burned low in the grate, the elderly narrator paused and placed a couple of logs from the nearby wood box on the glowing embers. After Bess refilled the coffee mugs, she took over telling the story.

"The philosophy of the Lodge has remained unchanged over the years. Not a single article has been written about the Lodge, nor an advertisement placed. Help always arrives when we most need it, and there are those who identify and refer families to this location. The original couple continued with their work through both World Wars, but society had changed, and the nature of the problems families faced also changed. The couple that founded the Lodge passed it down to a family that had been supported through a challenging period in their lives, and they, in turn, granted Charlie and me the privilege and honor of succeeding them."

Ian listened, fascinated by the tale. "How many people have been helped over the years?"

"We really don't know," Charlie answered. "You see, it may be the guest family that experiences a change in heart, but what they take back to their homes and their lives affects others. What they think, say and do influences their relatives, their work environment, their social contacts, their church and everyone they interact with in the course of their daily lives."

"So what you're saying is that the experience of coming up here, spending a few days talking about life and having some great food", Ian paused and grinned at Bess, "is all it takes to smooth out your life? I don't buy that."

"Neither do we," Charlie replied. "In fact, the experience here means additional effort. We've become aware of how we—and this place—affects others, and we realize the importance of everything we say and do. We also become attuned to the words and actions of our guests and what that tells us about what's happening in their lives."

Ian set his cup aside and waved off a refill. "You're moving a bit too fast here, Charlie. I've been to enough self-improvement and motivation seminars to know that while we can get all pumped up about a topic, or go through exercises to set goals, they're almost always of short duration. While they may have some small effect, generally the change is temporary, and everyone goes back to the way they were. People are programmed that way. Or even worse, we go and hear the speakers and immediately think of how this would help other people."

"Ian, what you say is a very worthwhile point of discussion. It has been my experience that many people go to those workshops and seminars, not to change who, deep down, they really are, but to put some gloss or polish on what they have become. To put it another way, some people do not want to change, but rather to appear to change. Change takes effort, and sometimes it can be painful. When you were coming up here did you wonder at all why we didn't have a bridge across the creek?"

"Yes, I wondered that, but I just assumed that it was too expensive or that there was some sort of environmental reason why you hadn't done it."

"Actually, the reason is simple, but we never realized it ourselves until the first time we faced that creek. You see, it represents the first barrier we had to cross in dealing with what we were experiencing thirty-some years ago. The creek is an example of the obstructions we all face when we need to change our lives. Over the years we have seen a number of families come to that little brook and make the decision to turn back. To them, that small impediment was just enough to stop them from making the deep-down changes they needed in their lives.

But let's go back a bit further. Do you feel comfortable telling us what happened in the courtroom?"

Ian looked over and nodded to his wife. Miriam leaned forward. "Maybe if we tell you what has happened over the last couple of years with Chad, we can come up with ideas about how we can help him."

Over the next hour, Miriam gave an account of what had taken place: how in middle school, Chad got mixed up with the wrong crowd and started having problems. She painted a picture of a troubled teenager who became increasingly defiant and rebellious. She told how he started cheating on exams, stealing from his parents, skipping school and, finally, arrested for shoplifting. From there, she relayed the situation that brought them to court—the use of drugs—and the action taken by Judge Stevenson, which brought them up to the lake. When she finished, there were tears in her eyes. "We just don't know what to do anymore. We told the Judge we would do anything, and we will—just tell us what to do and we'll do it!"

Ian reached over and took his wife's hand. "You see folks, we're at the end of the line with Chad. We've done everything and tried everything. If this doesn't work up here, the only option left is to let the courts do their thing and put him in jail. We don't want that, but there's nothing else we can do."

Twilight had descended, and silence had fallen on the group sitting in front of the fireplace. Charlie looked up and glanced at the others. "Let's go outside for a minute," he said, getting slowly to his feet. "I want to show you something."

As they rose from their comfortable chairs, they heard someone on the porch outside. When they opened the door Pete was cleaning up the butt-can. "Where's Chad?" Miriam asked.

"He's down by the truck right now," Pete replied. "We visited for a while and he's thinking over our discussion."

When Miriam asked Pete what he and Chad had been talking about, he said "We talked about life, and making choices."

"Perhaps I should go down there and see if he's okay," she said. "I don't think he's too happy about being here." She looked at the wrangler. "What was he like when you left him?"

"He's a young man in turmoil," came the reply. "He'll be alright out here—his struggles are all inside him. It's best we leave him alone right now, if you don't mind. He has to make his own decisions, and they're going to be tough."

"Is he going with you and Janet on a trail ride tomorrow?" the mother asked.

"I don't know, that's one of his decisions. I hope he does, but it's his choice."

Miriam's tone changed abruptly. "Look. I know you mean well and everything, but that's my son down there and I'm worried. He's only sixteen years old. He doesn't know anything about the bush and it's getting dark. I'm going to get him. He can think up here, or in his room, as well as down there." She ran down the steps and hurried toward the vehicles.

"Miriam, wait a minute." Ian took the stairs in a jump and ran after his wife. "I'm worried about Chad too," he said, catching up to her and stopping her. "He hates it up here and I'm afraid that this whole thing is a mistake, but I don't think we'll help by making him come to the house. Maybe Pete's right. Chad needs to make some decisions on his own. God knows he hasn't listened to us. And besides, is he any more in danger up here than he is in the city, hanging around with his druggie pals? Why don't we just trust Pete's judgment and let Chad think things through? Maybe he just needs to sit down there and see how he's been hurting everyone."

Miriam was still angry with Pete for leaving Chad alone, but her husband's argument made sense. "Do you have the keys to our car?" Ian nodded. "Well, at least he won't go anywhere if all he can do is walk."

Pete had been listening to the conversation. "That's not entirely correct. I left my keys in the truck."

"Then go get them!" Ian insisted. "Chad can drive and if you left your keys in the truck he could find them and take off for the city."

"I not only left the keys in the truck, I left it running." Pete said calmly. "And I'll tell you why. Chad has to make some decisions. We might be able to force him to stay here, even force him out on the trail, but we can't change his heart unless—and until—he's ready. That old truck represents a choice for him. He can take it and go back to town, yes. Or, if he stays here, it's because he made the choice. Not me, not you, not the judge, but Chad himself. I'm asking that you let him make that decision—it's a big one."

Ian stood quickly and glared at Pete. "I wish you had of discussed it with us before you did such a stupid thing. I know Chad better than you and, given the circumstances, it would have been common courtesy to talk about this before you gave him the chance to run away again. Look, he's leaving now!"

CHAPTER SIX

THE TRUCK WAS HEADING DOWN THE LANE, LIGHTS on. The three adults watched as it slowed for the creek, went down the nearside bank and entered the stream. They could hear the motor rev and it emerged on the far side, then saw it accelerate along the roadway.

"That is just about the dumbest stunt I've ever seen," Ian shouted, glaring at Pete. "To give a juvenile delinquent the keys to a truck and think for a minute he wouldn't take off! If you had asked us, we could have told you what he would do. I'm going to get the police and have them pick him up for theft. Now the only option is for the judge to put him in jail like he said."

"I'm sorry Ian, but you can't do that." Pete remained calm. "I gave him permission to drive the truck. I had hoped that he would stay, but ultimately what he does is his decision. I'm not laying any charges. In fact, I'll head into town tomorrow and phone the judge and let him know that we tried and failed. Judge Stevenson will accept our recommendations and not jail him. As to trying to catch him in your car—you can't. He's got a ten-minute head start, and even if you do catch him, what can you do? He doesn't want to be here, so the only option open to you is to take him back to the city."

"So, mister amateur psychologist" Miriam said sarcastically, "You're proposing we just let him go?

"Yes," came Charlie's voice from behind them. "Just let him go."

They turned and looked at Bess and Charlie sitting on the old porch swing. "As Pete said, Chad has a big decision to make and he can only do it on his own. We all want our children to grow up to be healthy, honest and contributors to society. But sometime along the way we have to let them decide if that's what they want to do."

"You knew about this and didn't do anything?" Ian asked in disbelief. "Is this part of your so-called helping that we were just talking about?"

"Actually, I didn't know about this, but I agree with Pete. Chad now has the unique chance to decide what he wants. No influence from a judge, none from his parents and none from us. It's all up to him. But I'd like to come back to what we were talking about earlier"

Ian wasn't about to let the incident get brushed off so lightly. "No we can't! I have a son out there in a stolen truck. I don't care if Pete gave him permission or not—we didn't. And I want him back. Now!"

"Why?"

That single word seemed to take the air out of Ian's tirade like a dart hitting a balloon. "Why?" he repeated, still fuming, but unable to answer.

"Yes, why?" asked the older man. "Tell me why you want him back?"

Ian stammered. "Well... I..." Ian stammered. "He may have an accident with the truck."

"Yes, he may. But that doesn't answer the question. Why do you want him back?"

"Because he's my son, and I'm responsible for him."

"Yes, he is your son. And your responsibility is to supply him with his needs—food, clothing, shelter, education, and the like. But is it your responsibility to make every decision for him?"

"We're not trying to rescue him, we trying to...to make sure he doesn't get into any more trouble," Miriam answered.

"But why do you really want him back? If you had refused to come up here, the judge would have put him in jail, correct?" The parents nodded.

"If he was put in jail, he wouldn't be with you at home. You agreed to a pretty brave action—coming up here. I assume from our conversation that you hope something will happen here to change Chad's life for the better. Is that correct?" Again they agreed.

"You two put your life on hold—your jobs, your comfortable surroundings and your social engagements—to drive three hours up into the mountains to a place you had never heard of. I know it was because of Chad, but why?"

"I think that's a pretty stupid question. What do you mean, *why*?" Ian asked "Because he's our son, that's why!"

"I don't mean to make it tough, but I think it important that you know why you're here. Yes, to help Chad. But why help him if he doesn't want help?"

Miriam was on the verge of tears. "It's because we love him, and we're terrified that we may lose him. He's our only child and it scares us to death that he might become addicted to drugs or get beat up, or even worse. Can you understand?" she asked, her voice full of emotion.

"Yes, we do understand," Bess said quietly. "You see, we lost our child—our daughter. We didn't know about this place until after she was killed. We do understand your terror. And it's vital that you love your son. Not for what he is doing, but for who he is. But it's also important that he grow into the man he can be. He's sixteen years old now—a young man. In two years he'll be on his own and legally responsible for everything he does. That's a very short time in which to grow up. What Pete did tonight is allow him that first step in taking full responsibility for his actions. Not easy for a mom, is it?" She asked with a smile.

"No it isn't." Miriam wiped at her tears. "So do we just let him go?"

Bess put her arm around the younger woman. "Yes. I don't see any alternative at the moment."

"I hope you know what you're doing, that's all," Ian said to Pete as they moved toward the porch. "I don't like this at all, and I don't think anything you've said so far—any of you—will change my mind."

The group climbed the stairs to the porch, but they couldn't go in and sit around the fire as if nothing had happened. Something significant had occurred and they needed the chance to talk it out.

"Do you think he might come back?" Miriam asked weakly.

"It may sound flip to say," Pete replied, "but Chad will only come back if he decides to. We'll be ready to go on the trail tomorrow after breakfast, and if he's here, he's here. If he decides that isn't for him, he won't be here. I sense something deep and truly remarkable about your son. I haven't had time to get to know him, but I sense that he has depth. Right now, things are off-track in his life, and he needs some time to make some pretty important decisions."

Ian wasn't buying Pete's logic. "I'm not sure where you get this idea that Chad needs time to make decisions. The choices he's made lately have put him in this situation. And I resent the impression that you know all about him. You just met him a few hours ago. Chad is a kid. Give him an inch," he said, mixing his metaphors, "and he'll pull on the thread until his whole life unwinds. I'm going to take a walk and think about what to do."

CHAPTER SEVEN

AS THE FRONT WHEELS EMERGED FROM THE CREEK bed, Chad pushed the accelerator to the floor. The rear of the truck slewed as the tires bit into the loose gravel, sending a spray of rocks splashing into the shallow water. *What right did that cowboy have to lecture me?* he thought. *Who made him an expert on me?* Chad fought the wheel and brought the vehicle under control. *If I have the right to make a choice, I'm not going to stay in the bush!* He pounded his fist on the steering wheel in anger. *It isn't my fault. It isn't!*

He used the heel of his hand to wipe tears from his eyes. *It wasn't my fault I got caught with drugs. If only that jerk Trevor had dumped them like he should have when the police stopped the car. If only he'd seen the stop sign in time—with cops parked across the road! If only Trevor hadn't lipped off the cops, practically inviting a car search—and finding the stash taped to the steering column.*

And skipping school? The teachers are dumb anyway, never pay attention to me except to make fun when I can't answer their stupid questions! And so what if I don't come home on time? What is there at home anyway? My parents blame me for everything. I can't do anything right for them. And besides, I'm sixteen! I don't have to stay at home. I can get a job and live on my own. Then I can do whatever I want.

He pushed the old truck faster. The intersection with the main highway suddenly appeared—signs and warnings! He hit the brakes.

The tires squealed in protest as he swerved onto the pavement, narrowly missing an oncoming semi. The driver of the big-rig watched as the pickup veered back into its own lane and headed toward the city. W*here did he come from?* Chad thought, as he accelerated to freeway speeds.

He wondered why his parents couldn't understand what he wanted? Why didn't they at least try to see things from his point of view? Didn't they know that he was having problems in school? Didn't they know that he wanted to do better but just couldn't? He supposed he loved his parents, but it seemed like forever since his dad and he had even a few civil words. He wanted desperately to please his father and make him proud, but lately his dad just criticized everything he did.

The sway of the truck and rhythm of the clicking tires quieted his anger, and his mind replayed the past couple of years. The first time he got in trouble, he hadn't intended to steal, but his friends were all doing it and he didn't want to be in with them, so he took a chance—just a CD, but when the police called his father, you'd have thought he robbed a bank! The store had a zero policy about shoplifting and he was charged with theft.

Chad still felt the embarrassment of being called names in public by his father. His dad wouldn't listen to his apology or promises to do better. He just ranted on about how this would shame the family and how his job might be affected, and how his mother would be humiliated. Not once did his dad sit down and ask why he'd done it. *Maybe I couldn't have given him an exact reason, but I would've at least had a chance to tell him things at school are falling apart and I can't understand some of the subjects. I would've told him how some of the kids make fun of me, and how the only ones who seem to like me were the other geeks in the school.*

Fresh tears came to his eyes as he remembered how he had worked so hard on a science project and got a C. When he brought the report home and showed his dad the only response he got was "How come everyone else can get a good grade and you can't? Are you dumb or just lazy?" Science was one of his toughest subjects and he had worked for weeks researching the topic, collecting information and putting it all together. Didn't he know how tough it was?

Before the lights of the city came into view Chad had been over every slight, every angry word, every accusing look he ever got from his father. His mother wasn't as blatant about it, but in some ways that was worse. She would just give him the silent treatment and tell him how much he hurt her. *What about me?* His voice screamed inside his head. *What about me?*

A couple of weeks earlier Chad had skipped school and watched television all day. When he flipped over to the Oprah show it was the tail end of a Dr. Phil segment. He had a group of people doing some sort of challenge, with one guy standing up. The guy was still angry with his father even though he had died a long time ago. Dr. Phil had asked the guy, "If you only had two minutes to tell your dad something, what would it be?" Chad thought about that the rest of the day. He thought about it now. What would he say?

I'd say, Dad, I'm scared. I'm scared I'm too dumb to finish school and get a proper job. I'm scared I won't live up to what you expect of me. I can't do anything right to make you happy, even though I try. I hang around with geeks because they're the only ones who treat me like a person. I want you to give me a hug sometime and tell me you love me. I want to go fishing with you. I want to shoot some baskets down at the park with you, like some of the other kids do with their dads. That's what I'd say.

The fantasy father-son conversation rolled through Chad's mind as he neared the family home. He turned into the driveway and killed the lights. He sat there, hands on the wheel, and closed his eyes for a second. Then a voice came at him though the open window. "Chad Jamison? City Police. Step out of the truck please, you're under arrest."

★ ★ ★

As Ian left the lighted porch and took a walk to mull over his options, he heard Pete and Janet say goodnight to Charlie and Bess and saw them walk up toward the stables. Ian wasn't sure where they lived, but it must have been close for them to walk home.

He was annoyed at Pete for leaving the keys in the truck to tempt Chad. It was almost as if they hoped that Chad would take the truck and drive back to town. Ian was also angry with his son. He wasn't surprised at his choice, but he was mad. He had hoped that Chad would grow up to be a model son, but that seemed an impossibility now. Chad was doing poorly in school, hanging out with a bunch of drug-smoking punks, and now this—stealing the truck. *Pete said Chad could make the choice to take it or not,* Ian thought, *but it was still theft no matter what spin you put on it.*

Ian walked down to the lakeshore and sat on a bench attached to the boat dock. The dog from the house followed him down to the water and tried to make friends. Ian shushed him away. He thought back to when the trouble with Chad had started. It must have been three or four years ago, just about the time he was beginning to struggle in school. Ian recalled seeing his report card and being angry about the borderline grades. He had tried to talk to Chad about the poor showing, but the boy had just shrugged it off as if it were meaningless, which made him really angry! He had grounded Chad for a week and forced him to redo much of the homework that had been sluffed off prior to mid-term exams. *Doesn't he know the importance of a good education? What has gone wrong?*

Inside the Lodge, Miriam had said goodnight to Charlie and Bess and climbed the stairs to the bedroom. Her mind was also in a frenzy of thought. Was she protecting Chad too much? Did she excuse his behavior too quickly, believing it to be a passing phase? And if she just loved him, would it change? She knew that she and Ian were sometimes at odds about how to treat Chad's increasing defiance. When Ian imposed some form of punishment, Miriam had found herself caught between the two of them. Ian would tell her about his frustrations with Chad, and Chad would complain about how Ian was mistreating him. She had tried to please both of them, and had even gone so far as to give Chad money when Ian had cut his allowance as a consequence for some transgression or other. But what could she do?

She flipped down the feather comforter and crawled between the soft sheets. She was concerned that Ian would lash out at these well-meaning people. That's how he handled problems—by attacking. That's the way he was with Chad, but it hadn't always been that way. She thought about the early years before Ian got so wrapped up in his work, when Chad and his dad had been great friends. *Maybe some time up here is what we need,* she thought. *If only Chad hadn't decided to take the truck, this could have been a holiday. They could have gone fishing maybe—Chad always wanted to do that—or even ride the horses.* Miriam still wasn't sure what they were supposed to do at this lodge, but it sure wasn't working out the way she had hoped.

As the house became quiet, past scenes came to mind. Chad as a newborn, then as a toddler, and his first day of school. She and Ian had so many hopes and dreams for their very special boy, but somewhere along the way it had all gone wrong. She wept.

Miriam had left the table lamp on so that Ian could find his way in the dark, and she was relieved to hear him coming up the stairs. *At least he's not going to do anything tonight,* she thought. She had been concerned that he might decide to head straight back into the city and deal with Chad immediately. She was glad his temper was cooling off—at least a bit.

They were like two strangers in that room, although strangers usually make passing conversation. But as they lay there together, neither of them spoke of what was heavy on their hearts. Miriam knew the silence meant that Ian was feeling stubborn about a decision he had reached.

Finally, Ian rolled to his side, switched off the lamp, and said firmly. "We head back tomorrow morning. My mind's made up."

CHAPTER EIGHT

IAN HAD PLANNED TO GET AN EARLY START ON THE drive back to the city, but without the sounds of car horns, sirens and heavy traffic he slept later than intended. It was almost seven when the murmur of voices and the aroma of coffee awakened him. He was somewhat irritated when he discovered Miriam had already dressed and left the room. He expected her to be in agreement in his decision to return home, and she should have awakened him when she got up.

On the floor below, the kitchen was alive with the preparation of breakfast. Miriam and Bess were ladling thick batter onto the pancake griddle as Charlie finished crisping slices of smoke-cured bacon in an oversized skillet. A huge enamel coffeepot sat on the rear of the stove. The sound of the coffee perking added a rich dimension to the friendly conversation and enticing aroma of a country breakfast. The table was set for seven, and the number of plates and glasses caught Ian's attention as he entered the room.

"Good morning Ian," Charlie said, looking up from the stove. "Pete and Janet will be down here in a minute. They're up at the barn with Chad, and the three of them want a good breakfast before they head out."

"Chad's back?" Ian asked, looking very surprised. "When did that happen?"

"I'm not sure, but it was obviously after we went to bed. I haven't asked what happened, but I'm sure glad he decided to come back. I heard about it when I asked Janet about their plans for today." Charlie lifted the coffee pot from the stove and held up a cup. "Coffee?"

Ian nodded. "Well...that changes things. I figured Miriam and I would head back to town early this morning and see if we could find Chad. You're sure you don't know anything?" He asked.

"No. I'm sorry, I don't. Maybe when they get down here Chad will tell us. They're planning on heading out before lunch. They have quite a bit to do, so they should be here any minute." Charlie walked to the window and looked out.

Miriam loaded the last few pancakes onto the serving platter and set it in the center of the table. She hadn't said anything to Ian except *good morning*. After retrieving a dish of butter and bottle of syrup from the cupboard, she stood with her hands placed on the rear of a chair and looked at Ian before she spoke.

"I don't know what motivated Chad to come back, and I'm not sure it matters right now. What's important is that he returned, and I think we should just accept that. He must have made some decisions last night and is willing to give it a try up here. I believe it would be a mistake to push him right now as to what happened. If he tells us, fine. If not, then I think we should leave it alone."

"I disagree," was Ian's response. "He took the truck without permission, drove it God knows where, and probably got into some kind of trouble. Maybe he's hiding out up here. Did you consider that? I think we need to confront him about his behavior right away while it's still fresh in his mind. If we ignore the stupid things he does, he thinks he can get away with it and will do it again. I'm not going to let him off the hook just because he came back. He shouldn't have left in the first place. This whole activity up here is to help him, and I think it's high time he realized what this is all about. I mean, I took time off from work, canceled a whole whack of appointments and probably lost a couple of deals, just so he could get his life back on track. If it wasn't for us, he'd be in jail, and I think he needs to understand that!"

Miriam looked at Bess and Charlie and shrugged her shoulders as if to say, *See what I have to go through?* Neither of them responded, and Miriam turned back to Ian to continue the argument. Before she could frame her reply the door opened and the others came in.

Flicking his battered Stetson onto the top hook of the coat rack, Pete greeted the group and headed for the coffee pot. Chad entered last and lingered near the doorway, as though ready for a quick exit. As expected, Ian went on the offensive.

"Just where did you take off to last night Chad? That was such a boneheaded thing to do! And with Pete's truck! You're lucky he's not pressing charges! But it doesn't change the fact that you stole his truck." He paused, but only for a second. "What do you have to say for yourself? Where did you go? Back into town to do more drugs I'd guess. With your friends! Some friends!"

Chad couldn't have answered the rapid-fire questions even if he'd wanted to, and he certainly didn't want to in front of strangers. Finally, his dad's rant run out of steam and Ian just stood there looking accusingly at Chad.

"Dad," Chad began. "I'm sorry I took off, but I did come back and I did apologize to Pete for taking the truck. I got back here a couple of hours ago and just slept in the cab until Pete came down to the barn and woke me up."

"Well *sorry* just doesn't cut it, Chad," Ian had reloaded. "Your mother was terrified that something may have happened to you. We had decided to drive back this morning to find you. Now you show up as if nothing had happened. Well something did happen, and I demand an explanation!"

"I said I was sorry, Dad. What else do you want? I'm back and I'm going on the trail with Pete and Janet. As to what happened—nothing! I drove to town, thought about things and drove back. I didn't get in trouble. I didn't see Trevor or the other guys. I just decided to come back. Is that so bad?" The quiver in Chad's voice revealed the strain he was under, and the frustration he was feeling with his father.

"Ian. Chad." Miriam moved toward them, linked her arms in theirs. "I don't think we should be fighting in front of these people. After all, regardless of why we're here, we are guests in their home. Now, Chad. I think we need to know what happened. We were very concerned. Both your dad and I were awake half the night worrying about you. Are you in some sort of trouble? If so, tell us and we'll help you."

"Look, Mom, I'm not in any sort of trouble. Why is it so hard for you to believe that I just thought I should come back? That's what you want isn't it?"

"What I want is some honesty here!" Ian cut in. "You take off in Pete's truck, then come back whenever you want to and we're supposed to welcome you? I don't think so. Not this time."

"Chad, we are worried about you. I know you try hard and everything, but if you'll tell us what's going on in your life, maybe we can help you." Miriam's words became a plea. "Can you just let us know once in a while what you're doing so we don't have to worry so much? If only you'd confide in us—is it a girl?"

"What?" Chad was surprised at the question. "A girl? Where did you get that stupid idea? No, it's not a girl. Why, would you feel better if it was a girl I was seeing? Would that make a difference?"

"No, not really, but I'm just trying to understand what's going on." Miriam's voice dropped to almost a whisper.

"I'll tell you what's going on then. I just don't like being around either of you. Nothing I do is good enough for you. You don't trust me. You don't like my friends. You think I should be smart in school. You never ask me what I think about things, you just make the plans and do it. I'm sick of it! I came back for a couple reasons, but the biggest was so I wouldn't have to go to jail. Now that isn't good enough for you! If you want, we can go back to town, and I'll do my six months. Is that what you want?" Chad was almost shouting. He turned and ran onto the back porch, jumped the four steps to the path and headed up to the barns.

"Now look what you've done!" Miriam reprimanded her husband. "You've made him mad and maybe he'll head back to town and stay."

"What I did? You were doing the talking, and he's the one with the attitude! After all we do for him! The clothes, the trips, the cell phone, the money for dates—everything! You'd think he would be grateful! He makes me sick!"

"Excuse me folks." Bess ventured, holding a plate in her hand. "I wonder if Pete and Janet could take some breakfast up for Chad. Then they can finish packing and head out? What do you think? Can this be resolved when he returns?"

Bess seemed to have a calming effect on the couple. Miriam looked at her husband. "What do you think, Ian? It might be a good idea. I know you want to deal with it right now, but maybe if he has a few days away it will do all three of us some good. Huh?"

Ian sighed. "I guess. I'm not too crazy about letting him get away with this, but at least we know nothing happened." He turned to Bess. "How long are they going to be on the trail?"

"About two weeks."

Ian was shocked at this. "Two weeks? I thought this would be only a day or two! What are we supposed to do while he's up there having a holiday? Do we go back to the city and then come back in two weeks when he's done his ride?"

Charlie had a suggestion. "Why don't you folks come and have some breakfast? Pete and Janet are putting some rations together for the trail and we can sit down after they leave and figure out what to do."

Miriam returned to the kitchen table. After a final look up the path Chad had taken, Ian walked past the table climbed the stairs to the bedroom. If he left now, he could be back at his desk shortly after lunch and do some of the work done he had postponed.

CHAPTER NINE

STILL ANGRY OVER THE CONFRONTATION WITH HIS parents, Chad pulled open the double doors to the stables. The dim interior matched his mood, and the sound of the hooves trampling the straw bedding provided a fitting background for his own internal voice. *Why do they do that? Why is it that every time I try to do something right, they criticize me?* From an inner stall a horse whinnied softly, as if answering his question.

Chad moved toward the sound, his eyes not yet accustomed to the shadowy interior. As his vision adapted, he saw a horse's head above the Dutch door on one of the stalls. The horse cocked his ears as Chad approached, and eagerly accepted a muzzle scratch from the young man. Chad stroked the cheek and neck of the large animal, and began to forget his anger. The horse didn't judge him, it simply accepted him as he was. It was a good feeling.

His reverie was broken when Pete entered the barn. "I brought a plate of breakfast up from the house," he said as he reached the stall where Chad was standing. He handed Chad the plate of pancakes, bacon and eggs. "Better wolf it down. I'd like to get on the trail before noon, and we have a lot to do before we leave."

Chad accepted the food, found a seat on a nearby bale of straw and began to eat. He wouldn't admit he was hungry, but he hadn't eaten since last evening at supper. The breakfast tasted better than he expected, and as he swallowed the last drop of orange juice he looked around to see what Pete was doing.

The wrangler was busy taking saddles, bridles, halters and other tack from a room off the main barn. "Finished already?" he asked, as Chad set the breakfast plate on top of a feed bin near the door. "If you are, could you give me a hand carrying this stuff out to the corral? Just put the saddles over the top rail of the fence and hang the bridles on the posts. We'll let the horses out through the side door as soon as we give them a bit of oats."

For the next half-hour they made preparations for two weeks on the trail. Soon the tack was hanging on the corral fence and the three horses, after a ration of oats, were led out and released into the enclosure.

"Which one is mine?" Chad asked, nodding toward the horses.

"Well, which one would you like? You seem to have struck up a friendship with Shiloh. He's a bit young, but shows a lot of potential. You'll have to watch though. Sometimes he gets *snakes on the brain* and goes a bit goofy."

"What do you mean…snakes on the brain? Has he got a disease or something?"

Pete chucked. "No, he doesn't have a disease or anything, unless you call an active imagination a disease. You've heard that elephants are afraid of mice haven't you?" Chad nodded. "Well, most horses are terrified of snakes. The more mature horses have learned what a real snake is and what just looks like a snake. Unfortunately, Shiloh hasn't learned that yet, so if he sees a crooked stick on the path, he may go a bit squirrelly. He hasn't learned what's real and what isn't. If you take this horse, you'll have to help him discover this for himself. Are you okay with that?"

"I think so. I'm not sure what he'll do, but I'll try to help him."

Pete moved closer to the fence, and Chad followed. "First, you have to watch his ears. You see how they're pointed forward right now?" Chad nodded. "Well Shiloh is listening to our voices. He can sense we're talking about him. Notice how one ear flicks back while the other is still pointed toward us? That's just him checking on other sounds that are coming from beside or behind him. That's called stereoscopic hearing. All herbivores–animals that eat grass–have it. It's a way of detecting a predator such as a mountain lion or wolf or some other carnivore that might be sneaking up from behind. Dogs, cats, lions and the other predatory animals don't have this ability. They don't need it. They can flick their ears back, but both move at the same time. Horses, goats, and cows can all move theirs separately."

"Wow, that's something isn't it?" Chad responded. "How else do they protect themselves?"

"We'll learn a whole lot more about the horses once we're out on the trail, but the other important thing to know, particularly with Shiloh's fear of snakes, is the way horses and other herbivores see things." Pete motioned toward the dog. "Take a look at Smudge. Where are his eyes placed?"

Chad looked at the collie. "In the front." He looked back at the horse. "Oh, I see, the horse's eyes are more to the side. Is that the same way with cows and goats?"

Pete nodded. "Yes, it is. You see this gives the animals that are prey for wolves and other hunters, added safety. They can see further to the side than the other animals, and detect a predator."

"I never knew this stuff. I thought you just jump on the horse and go riding. I never even thought about the horse being afraid of things. They're so big I thought they could take care of themselves."

"Mostly they can, but every animal has some fear in it. They can deal with the fear and learn to live with it. The problem is, though, in knowing which threats are real and which ones are imaginary. Sometimes a horse when it's young will slip on some ice and fall. Then, for the rest of its life it'll be afraid of slippery surfaces, even though it has become strong enough and big enough to handle those icy surfaces. The fear may have been real at one time, but the horse thinks it's going to fall whenever it's on ice. Our job is to help them overcome that fear so they can become good trail horses. It takes time, but with care and gentleness, even horses with big problems can become solid and reliable. I'm glad you took on Shiloh. He's going to need some special work and I think you're just the person for it."

Janet joined them, and they continued preparations for the trail. Halters were removed and bridles slipped over the ears of the horses and bits placed in their mouths. Janet showed Chad how to hook the browband over his right thumb and use his fingers to purchase a hold on the forelock. He was a little apprehensive about slipping his left thumb into the horse's mouth to guide the bit, but once he was shown how to place the thumb behind the teeth and the steel of the bit against the upper lip, he caught on quickly.

Chad learned how to place the saddle blanket so that it would protect against chaffing. However, getting the belly cinch tight enough was a struggle. Shiloh puffed his chest and belly out so the band seemed secure, but Pete showed Chad how to wait for the horse to exhale before tightening the strap, so he wouldn't be dumped from the saddle when he leaned over.

Loads had to be divided so the weight was distributed equally on each side of the horse, and bedrolls were tied on securely behind the cantle. Chad's mind was on overload with all the terms that were tossed around. Janet took time to show him the parts of the saddle—the location and use of the pommel, horn, skirts, fenders, and even what a saddletree was.

Chad shook his head at the unfamiliar words. "I may not know too much about horses and stuff, but at least I'm here."

"Yes, and we're both glad you're here—and going with us. We'll have some good times, and maybe we'll all learn something. Now, let's mount up. If we're going to get to the first campsite early enough to set up, we'll have to move along."

CHAPTER TEN

ANGRILY, IAN TOSSED HIS CLOTHES INTO THE SUITcase. *By what right does Chad think he can come and go as he pleases, without so much as an apology or explanation? This whole experiment has been a disaster, right from the start. Well, if Chad's going to stay here for the next two weeks on some cowboy stunt, so be it! Maybe I can catch up on some work without worrying about him getting arrested.* He jammed the last shirt into the case and flipped down the latches.

Miriam was stunned by the sudden decision. She was hoping the time away from the city would be an opportunity for her son and husband to bond again. *I feel so helpless. I try to be a good wife and mother, and a friend to both of them, but they're at each other's throats half the time. I wish I could get them to sit down and talk things out, and help them learn to get along.* She looked up and saw her husband hurrying down the stairs, suitcase in hand.

"We're going back to town," Ian said, crossing the floor. "There isn't much I can do out here for the next two weeks, and I have a lot of work waiting for me back at the office." He looked at Charlie and Bess. "I want to thank you folks for the great supper last night, and I apologize for Chad's behavior. I hoped that coming up here would make a difference for him, but I guess not. Maybe the two weeks away from his friends will be good for him, but I have to tell you, I don't hold out much hope."

"We're delighted you could come up, even for a little while," Bess answered.

"Yes, we are," Charlie added. "But before you go, there's something I wanted to show you last night before we got sidetracked. Do you remember?"

"I remember you mentioning something or other," Ian glanced at his watch. "But if I'm going to get any work done today I have to get going."

"It'll only take a little while, and if you could humor me, I would like to show you a place down by the lakeshore. Could you spare an hour? It's important."

"Well…" Ian hesitated. "I suppose I can spare an hour. Where is this *thing* you want to show me?"

Charlie pointed to the west. "Just down the lake a bit. We can walk there and it'll give us a chance to chat. After that, if you still wish, you can head back to the city. But, I do hope you'll decide to stay."

"I don't expect that anything I see will change my mind, but you folks have been such good hosts—and maybe the walk will do me good. Heaven knows I don't get much exercise." Ian set the case down and put on his jacket.

As Miriam watched from the kitchen window, the two men headed out on their walk. The sight of Ian with Charlie reminded her of earlier and more pleasurable times. She recalled celebrating Christmas at a ski resort. Chad had been about five years old at the time and just learning the trick of handling the unfamiliar equipment. Ian had been so patient as he coached the little guy on the fundamentals. They had spent the entire day on the bunny run, even though Ian was an excellent skier and would have preferred to tackle more challenging slopes. She remembered how the two of them doubled over with laughter and covered with powdery snow, dug themselves out of a snowbank.

She remembered times when she and her husband had played practical jokes on each other. On her birthday, when he had given her a new compact car but had worked all night to have the vehicle lifted and set on the top of their garage. How they had laughed together! And the time when she had gone to his office wearing a sexy dress and asked him for a date! He had just started the job and none of his co-workers knew that this brassy woman was his wife. Was he flustered! Even now the thought of what she did brings a mixture of embarrassment and chuckles.

And their quiet times together—the long walks, the stimulating conversations. But mostly she missed the joy. Miriam couldn't recall just when it had ended, but now it seemed like years since laughter had filled their home. A wistful smile creased her face as she watched the men round a bend in the trail and disappear.

"You look preoccupied with something. Want to talk about it?" With her quiet way, Bess brought Miriam back to the present.

"Oh, Bess, I was just thinking back to the wonderful days we had many years ago and how much fun we had. We seemed to get along so well, even though Ian was working hard and we didn't have much money. The jokes we played on each other and the dreams we had for the future. Where did it all go wrong? I know that Chad's been a challenge, but I think our relationship went off-track even before Chad got into trouble."

Miriam picked up a towel and began to dry the dishes Bess had rinsed and placed on the drying rack. "When I look back over the years, it seems as if we just kind of drifted apart. I know that sounds trite—everyone says they just drifted apart—but I can't put my finger on any particular incident or situation. No defining moment as they say in the books. Do you know what I mean?"

Opening the cupboard doors and stacking the breakfast plates that Miriam had dried, Bess took her time before replying. "Over the years it has been my experience that one of the first things to disappear from a relationship is laughter. When we think back over our lives the pleasurable times are the first that come to mind. We think of the humor and laughter. Have you ever noticed that people who are morose are those who have no laughter in their lives?" Miriam nodded. "I know this sounds simplistic and even a bit silly—sad people not laughing—but think about it a minute. We all know couples that are bitter, unsociable, and just seem to be waiting to die. They've let the joy of life slip away. Sometimes quietly and sometimes with a flourish, but nonetheless it's gone. On the other hand, husbands and wives who purposely seek out moments of humor and laughter keep their friendship intact. They share jokes they've heard, watch comedic movies together, recount humorous incidents from their workplaces and even play silly little jokes on each other. It's impossible to hold a grudge or to engage in criticism when you're having a belly laugh."

"You're so right!" Miriam responded. "That's exactly what I was thinking about when I was watching the men head out on their walk. I was thinking about the times we had fun together."

Bess put the last dish away and closed the cupboard. She poured another cup of coffee for each of them and motioned toward the door. Moving onto the porch, Bess pulled two old Adirondack chairs together, and they sat down. "I'm not a medical person by any stretch, but I've heard there's a chemical change that occurs when we laugh. The body releases endorphins that lessen stress, promote healing and give us an overall feeling of well-being."

The two women settled into the comfortable seats and rested their steaming mugs on the broad arms of the chairs. For more than two hours they enjoyed the late-morning sunshine, sipped their coffee, and got to know one another, chatting about interesting, yet inconsequential matters. As Miriam's comfort level increased, she began to share some of her frustrations.

"I'd like for Ian and I to be like we were years ago. We didn't have much—sometimes we didn't even know if we'd make the rent, but we were happy together. We did so many things as a couple and we always seemed to be able to work through any difficulties."

"Are you unhappy with Ian now?" Bess asked.

"It's hard to be happy when your mate is doing things that aggravate you and make you sad," Miriam replied. "When I get angry with Ian the last thing I want to do is tell a joke or even be cheerful. In fact, I think if I tried to tell a joke when we're having a fight he'd fly off the handle! He'd think I was ridiculing him. I wish I could get him to consider my feelings about things. Over the past few years he has gradually become more and more insensitive to what I want, and more focused on his job, moving up in his company and turning more and more into this person I don't really want to be around. I still love him and I think he loves me, but every time we try to communicate our concerns we just end up fighting. Lately it's been about Chad, but before that came along we had drifted apart. I wish I could do something to change him!"

"If you had a magic wand and could change anything you wanted about Ian, what would it be?" Bess asked. "I'm not trying to pry or anything, but you said you wish you could do something to change him. I'm curious as to what that might be?"

Miriam thought for a minute or two. When she looked up, her eyes were sad. "You know, I never thought I'd be asked that question. It's a tough one. I mean, yes I'd like something to change, but it wouldn't be really to change *him*, but to change our relationship back to what it was years ago. I'd have to say I want his respect."

"Do you want to talk about it? Or is this something you'd rather work through on your own?" Bess asked kindly.

Miriam was at a loss for a reply. Smudge seemed to sense her discomfort and laid his head on her lap. Without looking at the dog, she stroked his ears and considered the question. She trusted Bess and felt comfortable opening up with her.

"I've never talked about our marriage to anyone before. I always thought this was a private matter, and I wouldn't even discuss it with my family. So yes, I'd like to talk about it. Maybe you can give me some pointers. After all, you and Charlie have been married a long time haven't you?"

"Forty-seven years this fall," Bess replied. "But we had to pull together the whole distance. Later I'll share with you our toughest time—after our daughter was killed—but we've had to work as a team along the way."

"That's what I mean. Recently we don't seem to be on the same level. He comes home late, doesn't phone and tell me not to hold supper. He stays at the office more and more lately, sometimes even on the weekends. He doesn't even discuss important topics with me. You saw how he's planning going to go back to town, and he hasn't even talked to me about it!"

Bess interrupted. "When he comes home late or works on the weekends, or does something without consulting you, can I ask you how that makes you feel?"

"I feel abandoned. No, even more than that I feel that I have no value in his life, or that I'm just there as a convenience. To me, it shows a lack of respect, or consideration, and sometimes I feel he doesn't want to come home but feels he should—just to put in an appearance. I feel useless." Miriam was almost crying.

"So what do you do when you feel this way? Prompted Bess. "What actions do you take?"

"I tell him how insensitive he is. I tell me how that hurts me and that I have a right to be a part of every decision!"

"How do you say this? Quietly or loudly?"

"I admit, sometimes I yell. I maybe even call him names when I'm really mad."

Bess placed her hand on the top of Miriam's. "Now, I'd like for you to tell me how you think Ian feels when you yell at him or tell him how insensitive he is."

"I guess…I guess he feels that I don't respect him, or how hard he works. Maybe he feels that I'm inconsiderate or don't value him—but I do! Maybe he feels that I just wait for him to be late so I can yell at him."

"And when Ian feels this way, what does he do?"

"Well, he stays at the office more, and lately he's been working more weekends than normal and only coming home when he has to."

Bess lifted her hand and held up her index finger. "Let me see if I've got this straight. Number one: Ian stays late or doesn't come home. Number two: that makes you feel disrespected and undervalued, right?" Miriam nodded. "Number three: you speak harshly to Ian. Number four: now he feels disrespected and undervalued. Am I right so far?" Miriam nodded again. "Okay. So number five: he stays away more. Let's take this further. Number six would be you feel further disrespected. Seven, you would yell more. Eight, he would feel even more undervalued, stay away more, and you would feel he holds you in even lower esteem, and around and around it goes."

Miriam was stunned. "Is that what's been going on?"

"I don't know and it's not for me to answer. I'm just giving back to you what you have conveyed. But, if that's what is happening, isn't this cycle a bit wacky? I asked you to name the one thing you would change and you said it was for your husband to give you more respect. And yet the change you would most like to see in Ian is the very thing you are showing him. Or am I hearing this wrong?"

"No. You're hearing right. I just never realized that I was contributing to what I wanted changed. So how do I break out of this cycle?"

"Miriam," Bess said kindly. "It's not a case of breaking out of anything. It's really not even about our doing anything specific for, or to, the other person. What we really need to do is examine ourselves. We may not be able to control the other person's actions, nor may we influence in any great fashion what happens to us. But what we can control, and what we can influence, is our reaction to what happens. It's the meaning we put to things that affects us the most, not the incident itself."

"Now I'm confused. I was clear on what you were saying when you were describing how I am part of the ongoing problem with Ian. Now you're saying that it shouldn't affect me?"

Bess paused and thought about her answer. "No, that's not really what I meant to say. If you think back to the very first time that Ian was late coming home from the office, he may have had a valid reason. Do you recall any explanation he gave?"

The younger woman went back into the kitchen, returning with the coffee pot. She refilled the cups before answering. "You know I don't even remember the first time he was later than usual. It just seemed to creep up on us. No single incident jumps to mind. I know there was a first time for it, but it was so long ago I've forgotten."

"If Ian had been in an accident and injured, would you have become angry with his being late?" Bess asked.

Miriam spoke sharply. "Of course not! That would be stupid! I mean, there he is lying in some hospital and I'm angry because he was late for supper? I don't know how this fits with what you're saying."

"What if Ian had stopped to have a game of pool with some of the guys from his office and told you that was the reason he was late. Would you have been angry with that explanation?"

"Yes I would. Playing pool with his buddies is certainly not a good enough reason for missing supper and I think you know that."

Bess smiled. "Let's consider for a moment the two scenarios. In each one, Ian is late. When the time he was scheduled to be home came and went, you would have been irritated. As the hours passed with no word from him, your anger would have increased. You would have felt growing frustration over his insensitivity to your feelings and needs. You may have even engaged in a little mental role-playing. *When he comes home I'll say...or when he comes through that door I'll...* You would have viewed yourself progressively more victimized and disrespected. Am I on the right track here?" Miriam nodded.

"However the difference is the meaning or importance you place on his being late. In the one instance where he was in an accident, the significance you placed on his delay was considerably altered from the one in which he was playing pool with the guys. Nothing had changed about the time he was to be home. What changed was your understanding of his lateness." Bess continued her thought. "Consider this. There was not a thing you could do to alter Ian's actions. The only thing you could control was your reaction. That, in turn, would greatly influence what you said to Ian, or what actions you took when he did come through the door. Do you understand what I mean?"

"Not entirely", Miriam replied. "What you're saying is that as the time came and went when Ian should have been home, there was nothing I could do at that moment to influence his behavior. The only thing I could do was to control my feelings about his being overdue. And then," Miriam added, "what I said to Ian created feelings in him that were up to him to control, and so on."

Bess nodded and continued. "I realize this may be a bit awkward to work through. But it really is a very simple concept. It is we, as individuals, who decide how we are going to react to an incident or situation, not someone else. They may do something or say something that we are upset about, but it is still up to us—it is our responsibility. We can choose to be calm, accepting, tolerant, understanding, loving, supportive—or we can choose to be angry, upset, condemning, intolerant. If we step beyond our personal example for a moment, it might help us gain a better understanding." Bess could see that Miriam welcomed the idea of a different example.

"We all know people who become enraged over what we would consider a trivial matter. It may be a flat tire, a delayed traffic signal or a number of other instances. They have chosen to place a level of importance on the situation that we just can't understand. On the other hand, we know individuals who remain calm and cheerful even under the most trying circumstances. They too have chosen to place a level of importance to it that we can't understand. You see Miriam," Bess said quietly, "we take responsibility for our feelings. Whether we choose to be happy or choose to be miserable, it is we who make that choice."

"But don't Ian's actions dictate how I feel?" Miriam pleaded.

"On first consideration it appears this may be so," replied the older woman. "But, as we've been saying, what someone else does should not dictate the meaning we take from their actions. And, if we accept that there is little we can do to influence what another person does, we must accept responsibility for our reaction."

Miriam went silent as if searching her mind for a suitable reply. She was about to speak but stopped. Something was weighing on her mind, and she wanted desperately to share it with her mentor. Miriam had carried this burden for some time, but it wasn't until they arrived at the Lodge that she felt the need to confront it and deal with it. She was ready now, she thought, to share it with Bess. Once again she opened her moth to reply, but once again she stopped. Then she said, "Let's get back to Ian's being late, I'm not asking you to tell me how I could react differently, but could you give me some examples?"

"I'm always reluctant to give examples, as they can appear to be criticism of how a person is handling a situation. I'd much rather see folks arrive at their own understanding. But may I ask you," she continued, waiting until she saw Miriam's consent, "can you list a couple of actions you could have taken at the times Ian was late?"

"Well, I could have calmly asked him why he was late and given him a chance to answer. Or, I could have remained calm and let him tell me in his own time. I could have shown that I was glad to see him, even if he was late!" Miriam was warming to the challenge and becoming enthused. "Or, I suppose I could have told him how worried I was and showed relief that he was now safe at home. This would have shown that I wasn't prejudging his reasons for missing supper."

"And what do you think might have changed in Ian's reaction if you had voiced concern over his welfare rather than criticism over his late arrival?"

Miriam chuckled at the thought of herself in this role. "Well, first he would have been shocked. I mean, he is probably so used to my nagging him, or even yelling at him, for being late that he would have dropped dead if I was gentle and considerate."

"Do you think it would then have made a difference in the actions he would take the next time?"

"Who knows? Probably. But I can see where you're going with this. If I don't prejudge, and do show my happiness in seeing him, regardless of why he was late, then it may influence his actions the next time. Possibly he would try harder not to be late, or if he was, he might phone me. It's worth a try."

Bess stood up and looked around, then turned to Miriam. "I think that's a lot of discussion for one morning, don't you? I know it sounded like something from a self-help book at times, but earlier, when you were thinking back over the good times, did you recall how happy you were to see your husband after an absence?" Miriam nodded. "You didn't even think to ask for an excuse, you were just overjoyed that he was with you again. That's what I was speaking about when I said that the meaning we put on an incident is more important than the incident itself."

"I'm still not sure about this, but you've given me something to think about. I can see that actions influence a feeling, but it's up to us as individuals whether to accept or reject those feelings, isn't it? I can treat my husband with concern, respect and appreciation, but it's up to him how he chooses to interpret my actions. On the other hand, how I react to other people's actions is my choice. It's something I need to have to think about."

"Speaking of husbands, it's coming up noontime, and they'll be back soon. We'll put together some lunch, and if you folks are still heading back to the city, you can take it with you. If not, we'll have a bite to eat and decide what to do this afternoon." Bess carried the empty cups back into the Lodge and placed them in the sink.

CHAPTER ELEVEN

IAN FOLLOWED CHARLIE ALONG THE FOOTPATH THAT paralleled the lake. He was still seething over Chad's attitude toward irresponsible behavior. To take off and go back to town was one thing, but to get so angry when asked about it was inexcusable. *I don't know what I'm going to do with him,* Ian thought as he pushed aside the aspen branches that hung over the path. *It seems that more and more we are getting into these arguments. I wish I could get through to him how worried I am. He's failing in school, hanging with a crowd that will inevitable land him in jail—if it hasn't already—and in a couple of years he'll end up in some dead-end job, get some girl pregnant and never accomplish anything.*

Although Charlie was old enough to be Ian's father, he had maintained his conditioning through the years of walking and working around the Lodge. When the older man stopped on a hillock overlooking the lake, Ian was grateful for the break.

"I want to apologize again for what happened," Ian began as he caught his breath from the brisk walk. "Up until a couple of years ago you would have been so impressed by Chad. He was doing well in school; he was polite, thoughtful and really considerate. Then he just seemed to fall in with the wrong crowd and became more and more difficult to handle. I'm not sure if there's anything anyone can do."

Charlie looked out over the lake. Ian began to think that Charlie hadn't been listening. Then Charlie spoke.

"If I know Judge Stevenson, he would have asked you to tell him something good about Chad. Am I right?"

Ian looked at Charlie. "Yes, you are. After the hearing he asked us to give him a couple of examples of things that Chad was good at. What has this to do with what he's doing now?"

"Well, the important thing to remember is that your son has some good points as well as problems. The Judge asked just to remind you that families have a wide variety of experiences, and in a crisis we often forget that other members of the family have their good points. Those good memories usually involve interactions between family members. We tend to recall what they did for, or with, other members. Was that the situation with the examples you told the Judge?"

The younger man nodded. "I guess they were. But I can't see how those examples to help me understand Chad in this situation. Do you?"

"If you stay around a few days we can talk a bit more about memories of our kids and the importance of great memories, but right now I'd like to keep walking. What I wanted to show you is about a mile ahead and then we can head back to the house." Charlie started down the hillock.

Ian wondered what Charlie was talking about, but his quick departure and lively pace prevented any further questions.

The trail wound its way through the brush and trees bordering the water. Most of the time the path was within a few feet of the shore, but occasional rocky outcroppings forced the trail deeper into the woods. It was in the wooded sections that the quiet of the forest became apparent. The soft rustle of the leaves and the distant lapping of water on the shoreline were the only sounds.

Ian caught up to Charlie just as the other man entered a clearing. A dilapidated house sat in the middle of the plot. Weeds and wild grass had reclaimed what once had been a garden. The shingled roof sagged and bricks had fallen from the chimney. Battered shutters hung askew in front of splintered panes of glass. A few late-summer wildflowers still dotted the area but, in spite of their beauty, the overall scene was one of neglect and decay.

The elderly man lifted his hand to signal silence. A whitetail deer peered from the bushes bordering the lot; then, flicking his tail in warning, bounded into the woods. Ian felt the importance and dignity to the place, despite of its ramshackle appearance. He glanced at Charlie. There was a look of melancholy on the man's face as he glanced around the property. "Bess and I once lived here," he said as he walked slowly toward the home.

"What happened?" Ian asked as he followed Charlie. "The roof is sagging and the chimney falling apart, but I bet it was something in its day."

"Yes it was," Charlie said thoughtfully. "It was our dream home. We came up here the summer after our daughter was killed. We were searching for escape and when we found this spot, we knew we had discovered a special place. So we built this house and lived in it for almost ten years. But we had made a mistake, and it wasn't until the house started falling down around us that we realized our folly. The mistake we had made with the house was, in many ways, identical to the mistakes we made with our daughter."

Ian became thoughtful. This was the second time that Charlie had referred to a child. When Chad had run away and they mentioned how he and Bess could understand Ian's fear. And something about their daughter being killed? Ian said nothing, leaving the man to his thoughts, unfettered by questions.

They walked the perimeter of the old house, minding where they stepped. Shingles had blown off the roof during a windstorm and the protruding nails could puncture the sole of a shoe. A fascia board had dislodged from the roof overhang and dangled precariously above what had once been a flowerbed. Charlie had ceased speaking but the sadness in his eyes revealed a deep heartbreak.

"This was once a very beautiful home." He pointed at the house as he spoke. "Sturdy walls to keep out the winter cold. A tight, well-shingled roof to shed the rain. Shutters, painted green against the background of snow-white walls. A curved walkway of flat stones we collected from along the lakeshore and raised flowerbeds where Bess grew beautiful flowers. And here," he indicated the remains of a lattice-work gazebo, "here's where we would sit and talk about Elizabeth, and how she would have loved this place." He pulled aside the overgrowth and cleared the fallen lattice from the garden seats. "Have a seat."

"I haven't been back here for several years now," he began. "But I wanted to share this place with you. I want to tell you a story." He rearranged himself on the hard seat and then began.

"When Bess and I came up here, we thought we could make a new start. We drew up plans for the house, putting into the design everything we wanted. The size was right, the location was perfect, even the way the sun hit the porch in the evening had been planned. We had been married for almost eighteen years at the time, and just a year and a half after we lost Elizabeth." He paused, with a distant look in his eyes.

"We loved the early years here. We kept busy and helped out the couple that ran the Lodge. We didn't work with the families that came up here. We thought most of them were losers and deserved the things that happened, but we did odd jobs and kept the grounds clean.

"Within three or four years we noticed that one of the walls was cracking. We didn't know why, but it was a small crack so we just plastered it over. Then another appeared and we did the same. Soon we noticed that the windows were jamming when we tried to open them, and I had to trim a couple of the interior doors that stuck. As each problem arose we handled it, never once giving thought to the underlying cause. By the eighth year we were spending so much time fixing things that we didn't have time to enjoy the garden, or even to sit and visit." He placed his hands on his knees and leaned forward, looking directly at Ian.

"We then asked the keeper of the Lodge to come over and look. It didn't take him long to spot the problem. I hadn't taken time to build the foundation properly. I had been too focused on making the house attractive. I wanted people to look at it and tell me how beautiful it was. I wanted to impress them. I didn't place the footings below the frost line, and I neglected to place drainage tiles along the base of the foundation. Over the years the freezing and thawing of the ground and the buildup of moisture, shifted the foundation rocks. The floor lifted, the walls began to crack, and the roof trusses fell out of alignment.

"I got busier and busier just keeping the up appearance of the house. I never once looked at the problem of the foundation. I never considered that I needed to make some radical changes in the structure of our home. It never occurred to me that it was the foundation that needed fixing, not just the plastering of a crack or the re-leveling of a door.

"Eventually the wind would whistle through the walls and rainwater dripped through openings in the roof. We couldn't keep up with the repairs, and in the end we abandoned the house rather than take the essential step of rebuilding it from the foundation up. It still looked pretty from a distance and people wondered why we moved out. They didn't know that our home was fatally flawed. We had focused on the appearance rather than a solid foundation.

Charlie shook his head sadly. "I blamed everything and everybody. I criticized the material we used. I became angry at the weather. I thought that we had been shortchanged on the wood we used, and that the workmen we contracted were inferior. I refused to accept that I was at fault. I was the builder of the house, yet rejected responsibility for it." His voice cracked as he struggled with his memories.

In the manner that is typical of men, Ian stood and turned away from the older man, not wishing to embarrass him during a time of weakness. But Charlie recovered and continued. "I remember the day the last piece of furniture was moved out. Bess and I were standing at the end of the pathway looking back at the house. I remember saying how Elizabeth would have been so saddened that I hadn't built properly and that our home fell apart. It was then that I understood: this was exactly what I had done in her life."

Ian heard Charlie get to his feet and take a step toward him. The gray-haired man put a hand on Ian's shoulder and pointed once again at the house. "I had a very successful life while Elizabeth was alive— successful, if measured in financial terms, academic reputation and social prominence. I was quite wealthy, had tenure at the university and was on a number of charitable boards and foundations. I was rarely at home, and even during the limited time I spent with our daughter I was preoccupied with other things. As she became a teenager, the cracks in her life began to appear. I dealt with them one at a time, never once looking for the underlying cause of her unhappiness." He walked toward the rear of the property and dug around in the tall grass. With a grunt he signaled he had found what he was searching for. "Ever play horseshoes?"

The younger man nodded. "Do you have a full set, or do we just play with the one in your hands?" He walked over and began searching through the grass near Charlie. Soon they had located three additional horseshoes and began to play. After Charlie threw the first ringer, he continued his story.

"As Elizabeth's behavior spiraled out of control, I applied more plaster, hoping that this would help. To the outside world my family looked great. Wonderful wife, beautiful daughter, well-respected citizen, and financially well off. After a while my little girl got tired of these temporary fixes. She fell in with a group that gave the illusion of family, and that led, ultimately, to her death."

Ian could feel Charlie looking at him. "You see Ian, this house that was once so beautiful has now fallen into ruin because I neglected to construct properly. And I lost the most precious thing in my life, my child, because I neglected her. In both cases I was more concerned about appearances than building something strong and enduring."

A hush settled over the clearing. Even the sound of the wind in the trees softened. Ian was overwhelmed by Charlie's story, by his loss. He thought of his own situation. How he had become obsessed with the trappings of success. And now his son was on the verge of self-destruction. Although reluctant to admit it, even to himself, he and Miriam were on a collision course with separation, perhaps divorce. For the first time in years, he saw his life for what it was.

"Will you help me to understand?" he asked Charlie. "I've made a lot of stupid mistakes lately," Ian muttered. "More than I can count. I've alienated my wife, angered my son, and seldom have a civil conversation with either of them." He raised his head and looked at Charlie. "I'm afraid I've made such a mess they'll never forgive me. I need to rebuild my relationship with them. But how? I don't know where to start."

"Ah," Charlie replied, "that's the paradox. You see, one can't just magically change a relationship. You can't have a better bond with your son until you have a loving and respectful connection with his mother. And you can't have a loving and respectful relationship with Miriam unless the foundation of your own life is solid. It all starts with the individual. It's not external, it's internal. Just as I tried to fix the walls, yet left the foundation to shift, a relationship can't be fixed if one or both of the partners are unstable."

"Are you saying that I'm unstable?" Ian asked. "You don't even know me!"

Charlie chuckled as he tossed another horseshow. "No Ian, I'm not saying that you are unstable. I'm just relating my life experiences. But you did ask how you can rebuild your relationships. If you believe in your heart that those ties are sound and secure, and if you know the foundation of your family is solid, then you have answered your own question.

"But, if there's a place, deep in your heart, sending you a message that things cannot continue the way they are and that change has to happen, then maybe, just maybe, we can talk. You see, Ian, we all have hurts in our lives. No one goes through life unscathed. This short time we've been together this morning has been an immense help to me. It's allowed me to think about my daughter and share some very hurtful memories with a man who, I believe, can understand what I went through. On the other hand, *my* experiences may be of some help to you."

It was now Ian's turn to have difficulty with words. He hadn't expected this kind of talk from another guy—this was certainly a different sort of discussion. "I know I'm not the husband or father I should be." He shook his head. "I thought if I just tried a little harder I'd be able to make things better. I never considered that it was me who needed to change. That's frightening."

"Yes, it is Ian. In fact, I used almost the same words when I came to the point where I was willing to sit down and listen—actually listen—to the folks who used to keep the Lodge. Daniel was his name, and I often refer to him as the wisest man in the world. Because to me he was. He never condemned, never judged, only listened and spoke from the heart.

"The day we packed up and left this old house, Daniel met me on the same path we took earlier this morning. Bess went back up to the Lodge with Mary—Daniel's wife. We sat in the same gazebo as you and I. He asked me four very simple questions. First, was I living my life honorably? Second, was it a life of justice? Third, was it generous? Then he said 'Charlie, this last question is the most difficult of all. Are you living a life that is righteous?'" The older man picked up a horseshoe, turned, and looked directly at his partner.

"Ian, those four questions hit me like a sledgehammer! I didn't know what to say. He asked them with such compassion it tore me up inside. I couldn't answer *yes* to a single one of them! But I knew in an instant that whatever it was that he had, I wanted it!

"We talked all day and into the night. I couldn't break myself away from the depth of his wisdom. I was fascinated! It was if a bright light had been turned on inside me, chasing away the shadows of uncertainty and fear. What he had to say was so simple, yet so profound. He spoke to me of the foundation of a person's life."

Ian himself was enthralled. He had been sitting in one spot, not moving a muscle. The sun had traveled directly overhead, and shadows began to form beside the house, signaling the passing of noon. And still he sat there.

"No structure or life can flourish unless it is built on a true and unyielding foundation. The foundation for a building must be rock solid. It must be conscientiously planned, properly laid, and the mortar cured before stress is placed upon it. For if the foundation fails, whatever is built on top fails. In our life's journey, Ian, that foundation is our character—who we really are—our hills to die on, so to speak. It's what is truly important to us. It's more than our reputation, for others give us our reputation. It is more than status, for that also is conferred upon us. More that social standing, or wealth or fame. All those are fine, but they all rely on the generosity of others. It is only our character that we ourselves shape and defend.

"Let's head back to the house. I'm sure our wives will be wondering where we went. I think they expected us back before lunch, and here it is early afternoon!" He chuckled. "Ian, this has been an honor for me to be able to share with you some of the wisdom that a wonderful man once shared with me."

"I wish I'd had this talk when I was starting my family, but I guess it's better late than never." The younger man said as they made ready to leave the old homestead. "Can these be summed up in just a few lines that I can remember?"

Charlie smiled. "It's simply this. *Do what is right.* I know that sounds simple, but think about it for a moment. We know that we should be honorable. Why? Because it's right. We know we should be just. We also know we should be generous and righteous. Why? Because it's right to be all those things! We know in our hearts that it's wrong to cheat, steal, lie, and be greedy or selfish. Why do we do those things? Why do we go against the very nature of our heart? Again Ian, it is very simple. We go against the truth in our heart because we choose to do so."

The trail seemed shorter on the return. As they walked along, Charlie prayed for Ian and his family, while Ian contemplated the lessons he had been given. *Is this all there is to it?* he wondered. *Is it just that simple?*

CHAPTER TWELVE

THE BEAUTY OF THE SNOW-CAPPED MOUNTAINS HAD faded for Chad by the end of his first day in the saddle. His backside was aching long before the party stopped to make camp. "We'll set up camp alongside that ledge," Janet said, pointing toward a rocky outcropping a short distance from the trail. "First we'll unpack the saddles and take care of the horses. Then we can have something hot to eat."

The teenager was grateful for the opportunity to slip from Shiloh's back and stand on firm ground. They had ridden steadily for most of the day and his muscles were cramped and sore. He linked his hands and lifted them high over his head, loosening the tightness in his shoulders. Janet showed him how to remove the tack from the horse and hang the rations from trees to protect the food from scavenging animals. "Now what?" he asked when he had removed the saddle, blanket and bridle.

"On the trail, there are two priorities," Pete replied. "Taking care of our horse, and taking care of ourselves. Which do you think we should do first?"

"Well, I think I should take care of the Shiloh first." Saying this, Chad led the young horse over and tied him to a sapling. Soon the horse was munching on sparse grass near the base of the tree.

"That's not always the case," Pete said, smiling. "It's really about priorities. If the horse is the one that needs it more, then yes, it should come first. However, if the rider has the greater need, that should be taken care of before the animal. This isn't about a rigid or fixed routine, but about making decisions based on facts. So, what do you think?"

Chad waited a few moments. "Well, the horse is in pretty good shape. I've been riding him all day and he hasn't shown a limp or any sign of problems. But, other than being sore, I'm doing okay too."

"What about your boots and pants?" Janet asked. "They're all wet from crossing the river back there, and if you don't get changed into something dry, you're going to get a chill. If you think Shiloh is fine for now, maybe you should take care of yourself first." She paused, waiting for Chad's decision.

Chad's attitude had mellowed over the day-long ride, and his outlook had improved greatly. "I think next time I'll do like you guys and hook my legs over the saddle horn and keep dry, that's what I think!" He said wryly. Janet and Pete laughed. "At least Shiloh had a good drink," Chad went on. "I thought he was going to dump me overboard when he dropped his head in the middle of the stream. But I'm okay for now if I keep moving. So, what do I do for the horse?"

Janet took the opportunity to teach Chad the rudiments of horse care when out on the trail. How they used the upper side of the saddle blanket to give the animal a brisk, all-over rub, paying particular attention to the area where the cinch had been chafing the hide. And how to knead the pasterns, and then finish the rub-down with an invigorating massage using wild hay.

After gathering some native grass and placing a measure within reach of the horses, they finished their chores by adjusting the halter rope or *shank*, as Chad learned it was called. It had to be long enough for the horse to reach the hay they had placed on the ground, yet not so long the horse would become entangled during the night.

Taking a dry pair of Levi's from his pack, Chad disappeared into the nearby brush. Emerging a few minutes later, he was carrying his wet boots. "How do I dry these?"

"First we have to get a fire going." Having taken care of his own horse, Pete began gathering dry leaves, twigs and dead branches from the lower reaches of the trees. "On the trail Chad, one has to learn quickly and well. Believe it or not, nature doesn't care whether you do things right, are comfortable or even safe. Nature just is. So your task tomorrow night is to build the fire. It may make it easier if you watch while I make it, then tomorrow night you can handle it yourself." He demonstrated how to build a small teepee with the smaller twigs, gradually adding larger pieces. He then took a short steel rod from his saddlebag and unwrapped a piece of flint that he carried in a cloth bag.

"What, no matches?" Chad asked. "Why go to all that work when you could use a match, or even one of those disposable lighters? I have a package of matches here if you want them."

"I've always used a flint and steel to start a fire," Pete responded. "I've found over the years even so-called *waterproof matches* aren't very reliable, and if you run out of them, you're back to rubbing sticks together." Saying this, he stripped a ring of bark from a nearby dead tree, shredded the dry inner bark and placed a small pile on a flat rock. Placing the end of the steel rod close to the shredded bark, he struck several sharp blows against it with the flint. The sparks settled onto the bark and, by gently blowing on the embers, Pete soon had the makings of a fire. He cupped his hands around the glowing cinders to protect them from the evening breeze. After placing them at the bottom of the tent-like kindling, the blaze began to grow and was soon hot enough to begin cooking. Chad stood there, staring into the fire.

"There's a kind of unwritten code on the trail," Janet said, looking at Chad. "We divide up the responsibilities. Pete got the firewood and started the fire, so the two jobs remaining for the meal is either preparing the food, or cleaning the pots and putting things away afterwards. Do you have a preference?"

"I'll clean up and put things away," Chad replied, looking up from the fire. "Who sets up the tent and the other stuff?"

"We all look after our own bedroll and clothing. We don't have a tent, we just use a groundsheet, and if it looks like it might rain we each have a large poncho we can hang from the trees. It's not perfect, but it keeps the bulk of the moisture off."

"Oh, well. Hopefully we won't have a storm this time of year. I'm not too crazy about sleeping outside, or sleeping in the rain."

All three were busy preparing camp. Chad now felt more comfortable talking with Pete and Janet. He had the feeling that he was being treated as an adult. Any question he raised, from why they didn't put their camp in a nearby ravine to the method used to lay out the groundsheet, was answered. By the time he had completed leveling the ground for his bedroll, the smell of supper was in the air.

As darkness settled over the small camp, the trio enjoyed the meal Janet had prepared. It was simple fare, but the quantity satisfied their appetites, more ravenous because of the mountain air and the long ride. Chad took his own plate and fork, along with the pots used to make supper, to the nearby spring and rinsed them in the cold water. He used sand to scrub the outside of the pots, which had been blackened by the fire.

Having finished the few chores he had taken responsibility for, Chad put the utensils back into the assigned saddlebag and laid out his groundsheet and sleeping bag. He settled himself onto the down-filled spread and leaned back against an outcropping, feet toward the fire. For him, crackling firewood inside a ring of stones completed the setting of a camp on the trail in the mountains. But what to do?

"So what do we do now?" Chad asked. "No TV, no phones. No mall, and no guys. I'm not saying I want them. In fact, I kind of like it up here, but do we just sit and watch the fire? I'm not used to all this quiet."

"Yup, that's about all we do—watch the fire and visit. Anything in particular you want to talk about?" Pete asked.

"No, I don't think so." Chad responded after thinking a moment. "But, yes...actually there is. I was wondering how come there's no modern conveniences? I mean, I can understand up here, but back at the Lodge? No telephone, no TV or anything. How do you know what's going on?"

"Oh, we know what's going on. We have a radio we can use for the news, and people come up to the Lodge. They keep us informed on what's happening in the world. We've found, over the years that television and computers and all those wonderful inventions can be distracting at times. If we use them properly, they're a great help, but most people just kind of zone out with them. Most don't even remember the story they saw the night before. But, believe it or not, we use technology a lot." He walked over to a bag hanging on the branch and brought back a small instrument. "This is a GPS or Global Positioning Satellite receiver. I use it to check our position, and by logging in our route, we can keep accurate track of where we are. See?" He demonstrated the GPS for Chad and showed him how to use it. "This is one piece of hi-tech we use on the trail. I know you have something similar on your cell-phone but, here in the mountains, there is very poor or no reception."

Pete had more to say, much more. "As you have learned, even this first day, there's a lot of customs and traditions out on the trail. Maybe before we settle in and talk about things other than trail duties, I'd like to tell you about what we call *picking and packing*. When we were getting ready for the trail the last couple of days, Janet and I had to make a number of decisions about what to take with us, and what to leave behind. First, we decided not to take tents with us. While they would have been more comfortable, the added weight would mean that something else would have to be left back at the Lodge. We also decided not to take air mattresses, canned ham or soft drinks. These were choices we made together. But we also had to decide, as individuals, what we would take. Follow me so far?"

Chad nodded, wondering where the conversation was headed.

"The reason we had to limit what we would take was that everything has a cost—in weight, in bulk, and in usefulness. Some choices were pretty obvious, such as not taking Smudge. We couldn't carry all the dog food he would need. Others choices were tougher, such as a pillow.

It wouldn't add much weight, but the bulk would be a problem. We also had to choose what attitudes and feelings we were going to leave behind. What prejudices, or resentments, or lingering fears. For each one we had to decide to, either leave it behind, or, take it along. Those are individual choices—and important ones—because whatever we choose to take with us, affects our entire journey.

"And the things we choose to take with us are the things that influence the type of trail we choose. Heavy items, such as camp stoves, tents or canned goods, means choosing trails in the valleys. They're safer, of course, but the view is much more restricted. I'm not implying at all valley trails are no fun, but is that the purpose of our ride? Or do we want to see the farthest distance, breath the cleanest air, see unspoiled nature and study the night sky from horizon to horizon? If that's our goal, ravines are out.

"Likewise, the attitudes and memories we choose to take along can also affect our ride. Resentment, anger, and fear keep us from having the type of journey we are capable of. Symbolically, their burden on our heart keeps us down on valley trails. They weigh us down. They hold us back. We can't get up to the higher trails and see the beauty."

Chad struggled to understand what Pete was saying. Yes, he had chosen to leave stuff behind. He hadn't taken his iPad, soda pop or any of the other stuff he liked. "I'm not sure what you're telling me. What did I pack that I shouldn't have?"

"Oh, I'm sure you packed your clothes and things for the trail. I'm not saying that what you packed was wrong. Everything may be exactly the way it should. That's not for me to decide—that's up to you. No one can ride the trail for another. Each one must decide what they wish to take with him, be it a bedroll, a hurtful memory or a love letter from a girl. It's their call."

Chad smiled about the love letter. "No, I didn't take a love letter with me. I don't even have a steady girlfriend."

Pete got up and walked over to his saddlebag that hung from an aspen limb. He opened the bag and lifted out two knapsacks.

CHAPTER THIRTEEN

PETE WALKED BACK TO THE CIRCLE AROUND THE fire. Chad's eyes followed him as he shook the bags and held one in each hand. The bag in his left hand was quite old and beat up, while the one in his right still had the manufacturer's label on it.

"This bag," he said, holding out the left one, "represents the things we decide to leave behind as we ride the trail. We can place in it any item that may hold us back, delay us or make the trip more difficult. We can also put in any heartache or sorrow from our past, any destructive or negative tendencies, or any other feeling, belief or attitude we feel may keep us down on the valley trails and prevent us from achieving happiness."

Pete set the battered old bag near Chad, then moved to the other side of the fire, still holding the new, unused one, in his right hand. "This one represents what we wish to take with us into the future—up into the high country. We place in it those items that are of value to us. You'll notice, Chad, that it is somewhat smaller than the old one. This is because we place inside only the things that are truly important." He laid the bag against a rock, and settled down on his bedroll. He remained quiet as Chad looked first at the new bag and then, almost reluctantly, at the older one.

"Are you asking me why I decided to come back?" Chad asked, as he settled back against the ledge. The moisture from his wet boots create wisps of steam as they dried by the fire.

Janet and Pete had also stretched out and relaxed in the warmth of the fire. "Is that something you think we should know?" Pete replied. "It isn't important to us why you decided to come back, just that you did. I was glad to see you at the stables this morning. We'd been looking forward to spending some time up here in the high country, and having you with us just makes it better."

"I'd like to tell you. I think you should know the reason behind what I did. I know I should have told my folks, but they were so mad and pushy I just got stubborn and decided it was none of their business."

Neither Janet nor Pete replied. He had to determine for himself what he wanted to share with others.

"When I took your truck, and I apologize for that," (Pete waved off the apology) "I went back to town to see my friends. When I pulled into the driveway at home, a cop pulled right in behind me. He arrested me and put me in the back seat of his car. Told me that two guys had robbed a convenience store, and the store's surveillance camera identified Trevor. They thought the guy with Trevor was me. So they staked out our house and when I drove up in your truck they thought that I was coming back home from the robbery.

"I told them I had been up here at Lake Sandoza, but they didn't believe me. You guys don't have a phone, so they couldn't call here. I told them that you had given me permission to use the truck, but that you didn't know I was taking it to the city. Boy was I scared! I thought I was a goner. So they called the police out here to see if the truck had been reported stolen. It hadn't, but they still thought it was me with Trevor. Then the cop up here asked for a description of the truck, and the officer I was with gave it to him." Chad paused to catch his breath.

"He said they were looking for a truck that matched the description. I guess when I turned onto the main road I cut off a semi and the guy phoned the police. He described your truck and me as the driver.

What was weird was they didn't know the driver or the company he drove for, and he didn't leave a name or make a formal complaint—just phoned in the information.

"Anyway, the timing was perfect, because it proved I was out here when the robbery went down. It took a while to sort everything out, but eventually they let me go. I never even went in the house. I just turned around and came right back up here. I slept in the truck for a couple of hours before you guys came down to the barn. And that's the story."

"Well, we're glad it turned out the way it did, that's for sure." Janet said as she leaned forward and placed another log on the embers. "Think back. When you were headed into town, were you riding valley trails or mountain trails? Did the air seem sweeter, the sky larger and the view majestic? Or did things seem to press in from all sides and all you could see was a few feet ahead?"

"I was in the valley. I was so mad when I was driving I couldn't even see straight. That's obvious because I almost hit that semi! But now that you mention it, when I was headed back here, I felt almost happy. Maybe it was the close call I had, but I can remember the whole trip. I had the radio on and I was thinking about riding the horses and sleeping out under the stars. Would that be what you mean by riding the mountain trails? Chad looked at Janet.

"Riding the mountain trail is a personal experience. If you were looking ahead and feeling optimistic about the future, and you had no room in your head for anger, then yes, you probably were on the higher trail. But getting on the trail is one thing, staying on it is quite another."

"You mean even if I get on it, I have to go through this garbage every time just to stay on it?" Chad asked, groaning a little.

"Well, it does take effort," Pete answered. "But the longer you're on the higher trails the easier it is to stay on them. For example, the first time I rode up to the high country, I had difficulty. I wasn't sure what to take with me, and I had a lot of fear, being up here alone. But the more times I rode the mountain trails, the better I was able to judge what to take and what would just be added weight. So, in answer to your question, it's both yes and no. Yes, we have to make decisions all the time. But no, we don't have to have a crisis in our lives to make those decisions. It's a matter of choosing each time, and our choices are based on previous experiences. I remember I was angry at everything the first time I came up here. That was a miserable trip! I was thinking so much about me, I kept hitting my head on the tree limbs. Finally, the horse had enough of me and threw me off! Then I got mad at the horse! Rather than be calm and collected, I yelled at the horse. Guess what it did? You're right. It headed back to the stable, and I had to walk the whole way back!"

Chad laughed at the picture of Pete being thrown off a horse! He seemed to be the perfect cowboy. "So how did you decide what to take? Trial and error?"

"Not really," Pete replied. "You always learn, but what you must determine at the start is what is really important to you. Both from the things you take that will help you, and the things that may hold you back." He thought for a moment. "When you were driving back to the Lodge, did you have the sense that you would want Trevor with you?"

"No! I don't want anything to do with him! He's nothing but trouble, and now it looks like he's wanted for armed robbery. I'm just glad I was out here when it happened. If I'd been in town, I probably would have been with him."

"So you made a choice, even though you may not have recognized the process. That's what we're talking about—making decisions about what or who to take, including which feelings and beliefs. Does that make sense?"

"Are you saying I decided to come up here and to have a good attitude, and I decided not to bring my friends?"

"That's correct. Now this next part may seem obvious to you, but give it a try." Pete leaned forward and tossed a small rock that dropped in front of Chad. "If that rock represents Trevor, in which bag would you place it? The one you would leave behind or the one you want to take with you on the mountain trails?"

Without hesitation Chad picked up the nugget, opened the flap of the old bag and dropped it inside. "That was easy, now what else should I put in this pack?"

"That's not for anyone else to say, Chad. These are your decisions. We may rise questions or issues and help you work your way through them, but the decision will always be yours. If I, or Janet, or anyone else makes those choices, there's no opportunity for you to take responsibility for the outcome."

"If you're letting me decide what I can take with me," Chad reached in his pocket and pulled out a small plastic bag containing marijuana, "what about this?"

"Yes, if that's what you want. The only restrictions on the trail are that an item can't be a risk to anyone else, or a threat to the one who carries it. In this case, although I do think there's danger in using soft drugs, it's not urgent, so if you want to take some weed, that's your decision."

"I'm just testing you guys. I decided when you were talking earlier that I would get rid of it so..." He lifted the flap and dropped it in with the pebble.

The fire burned down, was stoked back to flame, died again, and was rebuilt, as the three sat and talked. Items that Chad thought were important to the trail he placed in the new bag. Over the course of the evening, they talked of many things: of responsibility, of accountability, of forgiveness. And the *way of the trail*.

Into the battered packsack Chad placed his last remaining cigarettes. "We don't have matches" he said, smiling at Pete. "No, that's not the reason. I just want to make some changes and this is a good time to do it."

"Are there any feelings you want to leave behind for now?" Janet asked. "Any particular hurts or angers that might interfere with enjoying the ride in the days ahead? If you want, you can also leave them behind. We'll be coming back this way so, if you want, you can pick them up again. This is a time when you can make some very important decisions. You've made a lot of them in the last twenty-four hours. Picking what to leave behind and what to pack along with you is not something that we often think about. In the old sack you've put some things that, up to now, you've been hanging onto. It's not our place to pry into your life, looking for reasons you did or didn't do something. But if there's anything pressing down on you and you'd like to leave it behind, this may be a good time."

Tears welled in Chad's eyes as his emotions began to surface. "I've been really mad at my dad the last couple of years. I'm not sure he even loves me anymore. He never spends time with me the way he used to. Sometimes I feel I'm just in the way, or that he's embarrassed to have me around." The words started spilling out. "I can't even remember the last time he told me he loved me! I try to do things to make him proud and he...he calls me stupid. He and Mom are arguing all the time—I think they're planning on getting a divorce—and it's my fault!" He began to cry as though he'd been holding back for years. He sobbed until his body shook, and when he tried to speak, his sobbing got worse.

Janet and Pete moved over beside the boy. Wrapping their arms around him, they held him tight as he shook and moaned uncontrollably. The inner torment he had carried so long was working its way out as he clung to the people who had patiently allowed the pain to surface. He swayed back and forth in their arms as his sobbing gradually subsided and the fire burned down to a glowing bed of coals. The mournful, distant cry of a coyote seemed to accompany the expression of anguish and love that evening on the high trail.

Chad lifted his head and looked at the two adults. "Sorry about that," he said, wiping his eyes with the heel of his hand. "I don't cry very often, unless I'm alone."

"It's okay to cry Chad," Pete said quietly. "It washes the windows of the soul and helps us see the way. It's okay to show the world the sadness inside."

"Can I put my anger in the old bag?" Chad asked, trying to lighten the mood. "I don't know if I can forget it forever, but the ride it might be easier without it."

"You can put in anything you want, Chad." Janet answered. "As I mentioned, we're going to leave that old knapsack here. When we come back, you can retrieve it if you want. But for now, if you feel you want to leave your resentment behind, that's great." She stood and brushed off her Levi's. "Just like the pebble, can you find something to represent your anger and put that in the bag?"

Chad sat and thought for several minutes. Then he leaned forward and poked the fire with a stick used to stir the coals. Moving a glowing piece to the edge of the firepit, he reached behind him for the canteen. Unscrewing the cap, he poured a stream of water on the ember, which sizzled and smoked as it turned black. When the charcoal was cool, he took it in his hand and, slowly, with a sense of purpose, placed it in the bag.

"I could probably sit here the rest of the night and fill a couple of other bags," Chad said, closing and fastening the flap. "I feel a bit relieved, even putting a few things in. I haven't felt this way before. But, what if during the ride I think about some other things I'd like to leave behind?"

Janet helped him secure the last buckle on the sack. "As Pete said earlier, picking the things we're going to take with us isn't a one-time exercise. Yes, starting our journey well prepared for the mountain trails is critical. But we're going to discover as we travel, that things we once valued, lose their importance. Then as we become more comfortable on the higher trails, we uncover things in ourselves—good traits—and we build on those. For now, though, you can leave this pack behind. If you want to put away other things further up the trail, you just do it."

Chad lifted the old packsack and carried it away. He would hide it, for it was his to conceal. If he wanted to take back his old life, his old feelings and his old character, he would be the only one who could find it.

CHAPTER FOURTEEN

MIRIAM WAS STANDING ON THE PORCH AS THE TWO men emerged from the trees. *Late again, as usual*, she mused, then felt a tinge of embarrassment. Wasn't that just what Bess and she had been talking about? Yes, she had been worried about the men because they had been gone so long, but did she have to blame Ian so quickly? *Maybe now is the time I should start doing things different* she thought. *Like Bess said, I can only control my own thoughts, feelings and actions, I can't control another's. So, let's give it a whirl!*

She hurried down the path to meet the men. As she approached them, Miriam could sense a difference in Ian. Oh, he wasn't really different, but something about him had changed. *What is it?* She thought. *I know—he's smiling!* She hurried to meet him, anxious to greet him, yet apprehensive as to how to do it. She need not have worried. When Ian spotted her coming, he broke off his conversation and rushed to meet her.

They came to a stop several paces apart as if by mutual consent. Not a word was said as they looked at each other. New appreciation was in their eyes as they moved forward and embraced. They wrapped their arms around each other; tears of happiness trickling down their faces. "I've been such a jerk," Miriam whispered, her face pressed against her husband's chest.

"No, I've been the jerk" he replied, holding her close.

"Maybe we've both been," she said looking into his eyes. "But we're not keeping score. I had such a wonderful talk with Bess and I need to talk to you now."

"I don't know what you women were talking about, but if it was anything like the wisdom that Charlie was imparting, I have a lot to tell you too." He linked his arm in hers and continued toward the house. "If it's all right with you, I'd like to stay up here until Chad finishes the ride. I think I'm just beginning to learn some lessons I should have discovered years ago. Are you okay with that?"

Miriam smiled. "I had hoped you would want to stay. There's so much I want to learn from Bess and Charlie, things about myself and about us as a couple and as a family. Yes, I do want us to stay. If Pete and Janet have even a portion of the insight that Bess has—and Charlie—this could be an incredible couple of weeks!"

"It looks like you two have a lot to catch up on," Bess called from the porch as the couple approached. "I thought that might be the case, so I packed a bit of a lunch for you. It's not much as we'll be having supper in a couple of hours, but if you want to take it with you up to the spring, that's fine." She returned to the kitchen, emerging a moment later with a picnic basket and handing it to Ian with a smile. "See you in a couple of hours?"

They carried the wicker basket between them and headed up the trail to the stable, then took the one that led to the spring, as Charlie had described. The elderly man joined his wife on the porch swing and took a sip of the lemonade she had poured for him.

As he settled back, he felt a cold nose nudge his hand. "Hello Smudge! Out chasing rabbits?" The dog danced around, wagging his tail. Charlie scratched the dog's ears, then motioned for him to lie down on a nearby rug. Smudge looked over at the mat, and then flopped down on his master's feet, hoping for a tummy scratch.

"So?" he asked, taking a long drink from the glass. "What do you think?" He set the glass on the floor beside the swing and looked at his wife. "Do you think they'll make it?"

Bess looked thoughtfully at the trail the couple had just taken. "Yes, I do. There's a lot of love there. I think they've been so caught up in the trappings of life, they've lost their way. They need some time to build their inner selves, and then to work on their connection with each other. Yes, I do think they'll make it. But I'm a bit concerned about something Miriam said—or rather didn't say. We were talking about how we determined our reaction to what someone else may say or do. I thought she was going to tell me something, but she stopped and then changed the subject. I hope she comes to grips with it, as I felt it was something quite important. If she forces it back inside, it could come between them."

"You know, Bess, before they even came up here I was hoping this couple would be the ones we had been waiting for. Ian was so receptive today and he seemed to grasp the concepts quickly. Oh, he balked a couple times, but once he worked his way through the cornerstones, I think he really took them to heart. I was so hopeful, but you sense something in Miriam that maybe she can't work through?"

"Well I'm not really sure. It's just a feeling I have. Even if I'm right though, I think she has the strength to put it right—whatever it is. We'll just have to wait and see how they respond as a couple and as a family. We have to believe what we teach, but it's their choice and their responsibility."

The elderly couple sat in silence for a while. Both deep in thought as they reviewed the day just passed.

"While I'm still concerned for the overall family, I do think they will make it with a bit of help," Charlie said at last. "We had that bit of help from Daniel and Mary, so I'm very hopeful for the Jamisons."

"I don't think you've ever told me fully what Daniel told you that day that made such an impact." Bess said with a smile. "I'll never pry into your discussions with him, but it obviously was of some great importance."

"It's not something confidential or anything like that," Charlie replied. "It just took me awhile to get it straight in my own mind.

"Daniel spoke of the four cornerstones of Life's Foundation. To live life the way it can truly be lived, our spiritual foundation must be secured at each corner. Much like the foundation of a home. There are four cornerstones. Each must be honored and placed into the foundation as immovable anchors. Together they form our character."

"How did you explain it to Ian?" Bess asked. "You said he kind of resisted at first, but then he understood. How did you explain the concepts to him?"

Charlie chuckled. "Actually, it was kind of funny. Initially, Ian couldn't quite grasp the ideas I was sharing—probably my lack of communication—so I used the same illustration that Daniel presented to me.

"I took a dozen or so small stones and laid them out in a square. And then took four larger stones and placed one in each corner of the square. I don't know why this works so well—using a physical prop to illustrate a concept—but it does. Maybe it's a guy thing. But anyway," Charlie continued, "once I put down the larger stones, he really got the idea of the importance of foundation cornerstones."

"So each cornerstone represented a principle?" Bess asked.

"Yes," Charlie responded. "The first cornerstone represented the principle of Honor. To be honorable, one must have an unshakable sense of ethical conduct. It is our *integrity*. The giving of one's word is a guarantee of our effort and will. Many times the word *honor* has been misused. Politicians, who are shameful, are called honorable, but that is not our concern. The first cornerstone of *our* character is to be men of honor.

"Is that the illustration Daniel used to explain the principles to you? I mean did he use the small stones and the larger ones at the corners?"

"Yes, he did," Charlie responded. "He actually drew them out on a piece of paper first, then used the stones. I wish I had kept that paper as it made it so much simpler the way he explained things."

"What were the other cornerstones that Daniel said were important?" Bess asked.

"The second cornerstone is Justice," Charlie replied. "To be *just* is, quite simply, to be *fair*. It is doing what is right, no matter the cost. People complain that *life isn't fair*. What they really mean is that nature is impartial. Maybe we don't like that idea, but the laws of nature conform to truth, not to falsehood or fiction. And impartiality is a key ingredient in justice.

"The third cornerstone is Generosity—having a generous spirit. Such a person is magnanimous and kind. There is a sharing with others of the goodness that life has given. It does not mean that the giver is a patsy who hands over everything they own, but rather that they share their lives in openness and love for, and with, others.

"The fourth cornerstone, and the one that locks all the others together is Righteousness. That means acting in accordance with divine or moral law. It is not to be confused with arrogance or ego. Nor should it be equated with religion. A truly righteous person is self-evident. He has a presence—a presence that emanates genuine goodness. God is revealed to the world through the deeds and actions of a righteous person."

"That makes so much sense, and it seems to have made an impact on Ian, and I think Miriam has started to see her husband in a new light as well," Bess said as she reached over and patted Charlies hand.

"They did seem different when we got back from the old place. To see Miriam running down the path toward us, I knew something wonderful had happened. I noticed the slight hesitation when they met, but, like you say, all we can do is plant the seeds. They have to work the soil if they want things to grow." He reached over and took his wife's hand lovingly in his. "Were we so different?"

Bess laughed. "Oh, my goodness no! We were so stubborn! I mean how long were we at the old place before we would talk to Daniel and Mary about anything more than weather and cracks in the walls? It was only when our house began falling down around us that we asked for help. We had the problem of not even knowing we had a problem."

"Isn't that the way though?" Charlie agreed. "We bury ourselves so deep in our own misery that we can't see a way out. Not because there isn't a way out—just that we delude ourselves so long. We believe all our troubles are the result of everyone else's actions, and the solution we say we want is the one we refuse to take. We're quite a species aren't we?"

The old swing rocked as the elders relaxed together. Finally, as if by unspoken agreement, they got up and entered the lodge. They were soon busy with the tasks of the place—wood to be carried and stacked, floors to be swept and dusting to be done. Together they prepared the ingredients for supper. As they completed their chores they heard the Jamisons coming up the front steps.

CHAPTER FIFTEEN

"We had a wonderful walk!" Miriam exclaimed, as she set the basket on the kitchen table and began unpacking. "It's so peaceful and quiet up there, and the spring is so clear! And the grass was so soft—just like a mattress!" She blushed when she realized what she had implied.

The others roared in laughter. "Like a mattress eh? Well we're all responsible for our own actions," Charlie teased.

"That's not what I meant!" Miriam giggled. "I just meant that Ian and I had a wonderful time—I mean we did things together we hadn't done in years."

By this time the other three were doubled over with laughter. "We talked! We talked! That's what I meant! We talked about things we hadn't talked about in years. Come on you guys, give me a break!"

Finally, Ian, wiping tears of laughter from his cheeks went over and hugged his wife. "I agree. The ground was soft, the spring was cool, the food was great, and we talked like we used to years ago. But you know what, I'm hungry. When's supper?"

"Well, if you folks are ready, we can sit down for supper in a few minutes," Bess said, looking pleased with the difference she saw in the couple.

"Good, we'll just go up and change," Ian said, smiling. "At supper, there's a couple of things we want to talk about. This whole experience is new to us and we need some help understanding what's happening." Miriam took Ian by the hand and they headed up the stairs.

Supper was a delight for everyone. Ian and Miriam recounted their experiences of the day, with Miriam telling Charlie what she had learned from Bess, and Ian telling Bess about the story Charlie had shared. "So you folks are going to stay with us for a while?" Charlie asked as he cleared the table.

Ian looked at his wife. "Yes, we are. Today has given us back something we thought was lost forever. So, if you're willing, we'd like to stay up here until Chad comes back from the ride. I don't know what he's doing, but if it's anything like what's been happening to us, we can't wait to see him. Even if nothing changes in him, the change in us will make a world of difference."

The foursome finished clearing the table—the men washing the dishes while their wives prepared coffee. In the manner of the first evening together, they took their steaming mugs and settled into the chairs around the fireplace.

"We love what's happened today—both of us," Ian began. "But when we were up at the spring we talked over what each of you had said to us, and about what's happened since we arrived." He looked at Bess then at Charlie. "It just seems that everything fits together somehow. Chad's taking the truck, us going for a walk, Bess and Miriam's conversation. Not that we have any regrets, but has all this been planned by some means or other?"

"Not planned, Ian—prayed for," Charlie said as he leaned forward. "Let's look at what's happened in the past few days. We were told to expect guests. By whom and by what means is not important, but we were expecting...someone. Judge Stevenson must have felt that there was hope for your family. That's what he looks for every time. Hope. Not vague wishes or pie-in-the-sky dreams, but real expectant hope. When he saw that in you, he believed there was an opportunity to provide an experience that would build on that hope. He saw the makings of a solid foundation for your family. It may have been faltering, but the ingredients were there.

"The second thing that was needed was faith. That was something we were able to see for ourselves. Remember we talked about you stopping at the creek on the way up here?" Ian nodded. "Well that was a demonstration of faith. Each time a family comes here we're always a bit anxious, because the creek is like a caution flag that triggers people to have second thoughts. Do you remember feeling that way?"

Miriam looked at Ian. "Yes. In fact, we actually stopped with the wheels almost in the water. We didn't know whether to back up and turn around or to just bite the bullet and drive on up here. We didn't talk about it at all, but I know Ian and I were thinking the same thing—what are we getting ourselves into? But for some reason, we just eased the car into the creek and up the other side."

"That was a demonstration of faith," Charlie went on. "Most people equate the word faith with religion. Although faith plays a big part in spiritual matters, it also applies to just doing the right thing. Somewhere deep inside we know what we have to do. Sometimes we're afraid. It's those times, like back at the creek, when we just do it. Not because it makes sense. We certainly don't do it because it conforms to our definition of sane and rational action. We do it because of this feeling that we should do it."

"And the incident with Chad," Bess said, taking over from Charlie. "Janet and Pete have an incredible way of looking inside a youngster and trusting their instincts. I don't think they expected Chad to take the truck all the way back to the city." She chuckled. "But Pete felt, after talking with your son, that there's a whole lot of good in that lad. And it did work out. Maybe better than we thought. I know he hasn't said anything to you, but I bet there was some hard thinking going on that caused him to come back here."

"Spending the day with each of you was a special honor," Charlie added. "During your discussion up at the springs, did you talk about foundations, accountability, and learning not to pre-judge a situation?"

They both nodded. "What this entire day has focused on is how we are inside. Every relationship begins with who we, as individuals, are. As I mentioned to Ian up at the old place, relationships between spouses cannot be honest, respectful or caring, if we are not honest, respectful or caring inside. We have to be right with ourselves, before we can be right with others. And, in similar fashion, we can't be honest, respectful or caring with our children if we don't have and show those characteristics toward our spouse."

"So this was planned—today I mean? Was it?" Ian asked.

"As I said, more prayer than planning. Both Charlie and I believe in God. You can't live up here and see the wonders of the universe without believing they were created. And you can't see the transformation that happens in people's lives without believing that the God who created this incredible world also has an interest in people. When we saw you demonstrate faith by coming up here, and knew that you hoped for something better for your family, we prayed that you would stay long enough to take a look inside and see the potential for change."

"So, when's lesson three? Or is it number four?" Ian asked.

Charlie answered. "If what I heard earlier is correct, you want to stay here and delve a little deeper into this whole concept of being a family. Is that what you want?" They indicated their agreement. "Well then, we'll start tomorrow after breakfast."

CHAPTER SIXTEEN

THE CLANG OF A STEEL SPOON AGAINST THE COOKING pot sent the Canada jay's screeching toward the treetops. Their searching and strutting along the edge of the campsite had garnered only a *scat!* from the cook, bent over the hot coals. "Everybody up!" Pete hollered, lowering the utensils. "It's after seven, and the sun will be up soon! Grab your grub or I'll feed it to the jays!"

The smell of frying bacon and hot coffee roused the remaining sleeper. Pete had been up for some time, as the fire had already burned low enough for cooking. His sleeping bag, rolled tight, leaned against his saddle.

"You guys always get up this early?" Chad complained good-naturedly as he left the warmth of the down-filled bag. "I thought this was supposed to be a nice relaxing ride, and you want me to get up in the middle of the night!" He stood and stretched, checking the sky. "Look, I can still see the stars!"

"And beautiful they are!" Janet said, emerging from the bush carrying a load of dry wood she had chopped from deadfall. "We always try to get to bed early and be on the trail soon after sunup." She looked toward the horizon. "That way we can spend the day riding instead of sleeping!"

"Yeah, but we got to bed late last night. That should mean we get to sleep in, right?" Chad worked his way over to the fire and poured himself a coffee. "Do you mind if I have a coffee? I don't usually drink this stuff, but this morning I need it just to get this cowboy kicking."

"Go ahead. Help yourself. There's powdered milk and sugar is over there." Pete pointed to several containers balanced on a rock. "As for sleeping in—nope! We follow the sun."

"What! You mean we have no choice?" Chad grinned, trying to get a rise out of Pete.

"On the trail, Chad, we just make things right. We adjust to nature. We stayed up late last night—and, by the way, this is life on the trail, whatever that brings. Remember we talked about how the trail doesn't care whether you're happy, sad, angry or joyous? Or on it, or off? It just keeps going. Same with time—doesn't care what you do with it, just keeps marching. So, in the spirit of the *way of the trail* grab some grub and chow down. You're camp cook tonight—and we're going to be hungry!"

Chad swallowed. *Boy, sure is a lot to learn on the trail* he thought. "So where do we go today?"

"We're heading up to the base of Baker Mountain. There's a big waterfall there, and a pool at the bottom of the falls. It's a great place to camp. There's a lot of animals in the area as well, so it should be an interesting spot. We'll have to press hard today, but we'll stay for a couple of days and do some exploring. There's an old miners cabin up there." Pete had finished his breakfast. When Janet and Chad had mopped the last of the scrambled eggs from their plates, they scrubbed up and repacked the horses.

The sun finally peaked over the horizon, lighting the distant mountains with the sheen of a new day. The Lodge lay in the valley below, still shrouded in darkness. The horses were playful at this time of day, but as their muscles warmed they settled down, picking their way in sure-footed fashion along the narrow path.

Chad's thighs and rear were still sore, but his spirits soared as he gained confidence in his horse and in the belief that his problems remained in the bag back at camp. Lunch was taken at a widening of the trail. After a cold snack of beef jerky, biscuits and water, the riders remounted and continued climbing the ever-narrowing path, allowing the animals their head in picking their way through icy creeks and along the switchbacks as they rode higher.

By late afternoon, even the veteran riders were ready to call it a day. The final leg of the trail led them through a narrow, heavily timbered, canyon. The sound of a waterfall grew steadily louder as they neared their chosen campsite. As they wound their way along the overgrown trail, Chad could feel the fine spray hanging in the air, mingled with fragrant scent of ponderosa pine.

The sight and sound of the cascade as it plummeted from high above and collided with the boulders below was incredible. Chad sat astride his horse and stared in wonder.

"Pretty awesome, isn't it?" Pete asked, riding up beside him. "Only a few people ever come up here. As you can see from the trail, it's pretty well overgrown. There's just us and a few others who know about this place, so keep it quiet, okay?" He faked a southern drawl. "We don't want any of them thar city slickers comin' up and disturbin' things, do we?"

Chad laughed. "No, we don' want 'em messin' arou' up here—jes wanna keep it for ourselves," He slid off the back of the horse, taking the reins and leading the horse to the edge of the pool for a drink. "You know Pete, up until now I never gave a thought to what an incredible country this is. These mountains are something! Today as I was riding, I started to understand what you were talking about—riding the higher trails and all."

"It is an incredible place. These higher trails are seldom traveled. Only a few people actually look up and see the beauty around them. But, like we were discussing last night, most people are carrying so much baggage they can't get to the higher trails. They get stuck in the valleys and sometimes never get out. I'm glad you get to see this."

Setting up camp was easier that evening. The horses were given their rub, then staked out near the pond below the falls. Janet gathered the wood and built the fire. Chad gave his full attention to preparing the meal and, although he occasionally looked to Janet and Pete for help, he was left alone. He had little cooking experience so he selected a simple meal of macaroni and cheese. He was ravenous and guessed the others were as well, so while the food was simple, he made enough for a group of ten!

When the cleanup was completed, the three relaxed, leaning against their bedrolls. A large, shiny, black bird landed several feet away from the resting group, and then boldly strutted toward the pack containing the food. "Boy, that's one huge crow!" Chad said, as the bird began pulling at the flap.

"Actually, it's a raven," Janet pointed out. "It has quite a reputation for getting into mischief. It's quite a bit larger than the common crow, and a Haida legend has it that his tricks gave early man the essentials for survival. A lot of stories about the raven have been handed down through the various native tribes. If you like, Pete can tell you some of them."

"I'd like to hear some, just as long as they don't have some moral that I have to learn." Chad laughed at his own remark. "I don't think I can handle any more changes in my life right now."

CHAPTER SEVENTEEN

WHAT AMAZED IAN AND MIRIAM WAS THAT IN SPITE of almost a week of very intensive learning, neither of them had the feeling of being in a seminar or participating in a program. Charlie was a teacher in the Socratic method, asking questions that stimulated discussion or making observations and then challenging his own precepts. On the other hand, Bess was the wise elder, dispensing wisdom in stories, legends and spiritual references. Each day after breakfast the foursome engaged in energetic conversation, examining the previous day's topics and refreshing their memories of the lessons learned. By mid-morning each day, they tackled a new concept. What surprised the learners was the simplicity of the information. The ideas weren't new, but applying them on a personal level was exciting.

"We've spent the better part of the past few days discussing who we are inside: what our hearts are like in relation to our thoughts, attitudes and actions, and the importance of being at peace within." They were seated in the shade of an old weeping birch, and Bess was reviewing previous topics.

"There's an old saying that *actions speak louder than words*. We take this maxim to mean that we say one thing but do another, and, in many instances, this is just what occurs. We violate society's codes of behavior. We proclaim honesty yet cheat on taxes. We decry moral decay yet betray those we love. However, there are deeper roots to the proverb, and they have significance in our relationship with others. I'm referring to the violation of our inner code of ethics." Miriam and Ian waited for Bess to continue.

"An honest person has no need to declare his or her honesty—they just are. A moral person does not proclaim to the world *Look how honest I am!* It's part of their inner code. The word *code* comes from a Latin root, meaning the trunk of the tree. It is solid and permanent, not swaying and bending with each breath of wind. The tree does not say *I am immovable* it just is!

"And so it is with the individual. Each one has established inner codes. I believe, Ian," Bess said, looking at him, "that codes—or cornerstones—formed the substance of your conversation with Charlie up at the old place?" Ian nodded.

"You see we cannot be true to others unless, and until, we are true to ourselves. And to be true to ourselves is not to be selfish, but rather to do what is right. Being selfish is the action we take when we place ourselves at an advantage over others. In those instances, we decide not on what is right, but what is right for us."

Charlie added a thought. "The last few days we have talked about doing right, about making decisions in our lives that are honorable, and that reflect to the world just who we are deep inside. That inner self is what we are made of. I cannot honor my spouse if I am not an honorable person. My spouse cannot trust me if I am untrustworthy. A good husband does not seek to prove he is a good husband, nor does he try to find things to do that show just how good a husband he is. He does things because they are the right things to do, and because he is a good husband. If he does right, honorable and just things, he will be a good husband. Not because he *tries*, but because he *does*.

"In the same fashion, a father who is doing what is right as a father, does not think to himself *What can I do that will make me look like I'm a good father?* He will actually do the things that a good father does. I know the difference is subtle, yet it has incredible consequences in the relationship he has with his children."

Bess concluded the thought. "Everything begins inside. And without being at peace inside, we cannot be at peace with our spouse or our children."

Ian and Miriam were trying to digested the wisdom. "I see how what we are and what we do impacts others," Miriam said turning to Ian. "Bess and I discussed that a couple of days ago." She turned to Bess again. "But how is it that when our family started going off track we weren't able to put it back on course quickly? I mean, we wanted to, but everything I did, Ian did and Chad did, seemed to make it worse."

Bess appreciated the opportunity to discuss Miriam's quandary. "Imagine, if you will, that a family is a human body. It is a complete unit, composed of many individual and distinct parts. Each part has a role to play but something happening to one part, impacts the whole body. A wrist is sprained. At first the pain is localized in that area, although the rest of the body quickly identifies that a member, or part, is in distress. The other hand reaches across and cradles the injured limb. The body bends over to shield it. The pain prompts the voice to moan and the eyes to water. The other parts are in sympathy with the injured arm. Likewise, when a child or spouse is injured, the entire family is impacted. But it doesn't stop there. And I think this may help to answer your question.

"Consider how the entire body is in sympathy with the sprain. As the day's pass, the hurt lessens—not because the other parts absorb the pain, but because the sprain has begun to heal. However, if it is not treated, the entire body will feel the pain again—in other areas. The other arm grows weary of holding the injured wrist. The shoulders slump from awkward lifting positions. Repair is needed, and it is the mind that makes the decision to go to the emergency clinic, where a cast is placed around it, medication is provided, and a sling is fastened around the neck. Why does the mind make the decision to repair the injury and make the body whole again?"

"Because it's the right thing to do?" Ian answered.

"Go to the head of the class!" Charlie laughed. "And when one part of the family is hurting, the entire family hurts. Healing must begin. That requires a decision. And in the analogy Bess used, the body also learned from the experience not to allow the wrist to get in that situation again!"

As Bess explained the injured-limb analogy, she noticed Miriam gradually withdrawing from the discussion. For some reason this particular example was causing her to pull back. What it was and how it would affect the family could not be dealt with here. "Maybe we'll take a bit of a break," Bess said, standing. "Charlie and I will just visit a while. If you'd like a very pretty walk, there's a path near the stables, not far from the spring where you went before. A little stream comes down and cuts across the trail. The large rocks that border the path were placed by guests who stayed here at the Lodge. There are no markers or indicators to tell us what the stones mean, but each represents a burden the guest wanted to leave behind. It's a special place."

Ian and Miriam left the Lodge and walked up the trail toward the spring, but somehow they missed the path Bess had described. Within minutes they realized they had gone past the fork, and began to retrace their steps. As they walked along, Ian avoided commented on the decision to take a break. He had sensed Miriam's distress during the discussion and wanted to give her space. "There it is!" He pointed out the path as it came into view.

Pushing aside the lower branches, Ian allowed Miriam to lead the way along the path that led to the spring. "The air is cooler here," she said, glancing back at Ian. It wasn't long before they saw the first of the *leaving stones*. Each rock was unique, and it became obvious that they had been chosen and placed with purpose. One was of granite, another of quartz, and yet another of the more common sandstone. They stood in silence, feeling at peace, as though they were visiting a sacred place.

They became aware of the murmur of the tiny brook as it crossed under the pathway, and saw the imprint of a deer's hoof in the damp soil beside the water. Sunlight filtered through the branches overhead, and a breeze stirred the leaves. Miriam took Ian's hand in hers and led him toward the brook. She took off her shoes, placed them on the ground and sat on the bank, resting against a tree. Ian lowered himself carefully and sat beside her. He watched as she stretched her legs and dipped her feet in the clear, cold water.

After a while Miriam began to share what was on her mind. "This has been an incredible week for me," she said slowly. "I've so enjoyed the time we've spent with Charlie and Bess—Bess in particular. I've learned so much! But when they talked about how a family begins to hurt and doesn't deal with it, I began to see the problems I've been causing." Ian started to say something, but she placed a finger against his lips. "No, please, let me finish. I think I spotted our difficulty with Chad before you did. I noticed his behavior change, but I didn't do anything about it. I think I was afraid, yet at the same time I was just hoping everything would pass and...and things would get back to normal."

Tears welled up in Miriam's eyes. She turned to her husband, taking his hand in both of hers. "It's so clear to me now that I was a part of Chad's problem. I was so scared; I didn't know what else to do. I know I should have told you, but I was afraid you would get angry. I should have realized that you care about him as much as I do!" She began to cry.

"What are you talking about?" Ian asked gently. "I was about to say that I was the problem. I knew Chad was on a collision course with disaster, yet I was too stubborn to admit our family needed help."

"Oh, Ian. I'm so sorry the way things happened. Chad would tell me a story and I wanted to believe him so bad that when he would tell me he owed a friend some money, or he needed to buy something for school, even though, deep down, I had doubts, I gave him money. And I realize now he was using that money for drugs! I was trying to protect him and instead I was just letting the pain continue until it started hurting the whole family!"

"It's okay honey. I think both of us have enough guilt to last a while. What's important is that we're doing something about it. But I think it also illustrates something that Charlie said: that one spouse can't trust the other if that person is not trustworthy, or something like that. I guess I wasn't being trustworthy. That, in turn prevented you from sharing with me your concerns about Chad. And many times I didn't share my fears with you." He continued holding her hands. "This time, I'm not going to tell you I'll be a better husband or a better father. I'll be one."

They continued talking, each revealing for the first time their anguish and despair. "I think," Ian began, "that maybe we should leave this behind. I don't mean this spot; I mean the problems of the past. We have to learn from it and grow, of course, but I believe if we're making a new start, what we did—or didn't do—over the past few years shouldn't be a burden from now on."

Miriam nodded. "I like that. If we don't leave in the past all the problems we've dealt with, we'll end up carrying an awful heavy load into the future. Bess said these stones are symbols of burdens and cares that other families have decided to leave behind—as memorials, sort of. Maybe we should do that."

"I love the idea!" Ian said, scrambling to his feet. "But let's find one that really represents, for us, what we're leaving behind. Okay?"

"Yes," Miriam agreed, getting to her feet. "What do you have in mind?"

"I'm not sure. Let's walk around and see if something sort of speaks to us." They moved off into the trees bordering the stream. As they moved along, pushing aside branches, stepping over fallen logs and stumbling over exposed roots and rocks, their hearts felt lighter. One of them would find a rock and extol its merit, only to set is aside; then the other would discover a stone and lobby for its placement. They were so thoroughly engrossed in the search that they almost forgot the serious nature of their quest. At last they agreed on a boulder—so large it required their combined strength to roll it out of the bush and position it alongside the trail, where they sat catching their breath.

Ian placed his hand on the rock. "We will let this rock represent, for us, the past." Miriam laid her hand on top of his. "I agree. We learn from the lessons of yesterday, apply them today, so that our future may be better." With a last pat on the top of the large stone, they got to their feet.

"Now that we've worked on the past, how do we continue to work together on the future?" Miriam asked. "Maybe we should talk it over with Charlie and Bess."

Together they worked their way back down the pathway to the Lodge. Bess had laid out a snack and was pouring lemonade into four glasses as they came in. She had a knack for knowing exactly what was needed.

After a long drink of lemonade, Ian turned to the older couple. "We read so many times, and hear so often, how marriage is something that must be worked on all the time. How do you folks keep your marriage working so well? You've been married forty-seven years, lost a child, gave up your position, lost your house? Why didn't it fall apart?"

"Our marriage wasn't perfect—none are," Charlie admitted. "And you're right, Ian, the common misconception is that you have to work at it. Work implies labor and effort. We prefer to think of our marriage as a treasure. We're always on the lookout for things to add to our fortune. Shared experiences, inside jokes, challenging ideas, and new friends—all add to our storehouse of wealth.

"And that treasure we call marriage is something that must be guarded. It's not really something to be *worked at,* I don't think, but rather a relationship to be shared. All relationships have ups and downs, and we have to recognize that. What's important is that both wife and husband have made vows to love, honor, trust and support each other through thick and thin. Those promises are much more than just words; they are a commitment. When one says *in sickness and in health,* there is an implication that there will be illness, and when one vows to support another *through good times and bad,* we know that bad times will come and that you will stick together. To say one will *love, honor and cherish* is to give a promise to the world that you will keep that promise.

"Is there any situation where a divorce is warranted?" Charlie paused, letting the question register. "Yes, I believe there is, but not as often or as easily as it happens today. Like the illustration with the injured wrist and getting medical attention, there are occasions when a physician recommends an amputation. If the hand is so damaged that it threatens the entire body, not with pain but with death, then it is necessary to have that operation. But that operation—and divorce—should be the last alternative."

"You know," Miriam confided, "when we began having problems as a family, one of the alternatives we looked at was divorce. We tried counseling, we tried communicating, we tried just about everything. Finally, we said the D-word. It was scary because we had both been thinking it, but not saying it, and once it was out in the open we could make plans. It just seemed so easy!"

"And another thing," Ian added. "We stopped going out. We stopped seeing friends, or if we did, we visited them very briefly out of duty. When you said that marriage is a treasure to be shared and protected, it strikes me that we were doing the exact opposite. We were allowing it be ransacked—by lawyers, our bosses, our individual friends and even ourselves. We didn't treasure it, and we did nothing to protect it."

Charlie looked through the leaves that shaded them. "It's just about noon. Why don't we have lunch and then the rest of the afternoon is yours? We've covered a lot this morning and perhaps the two of you have more to discuss? Bess and I will—maybe we'll take the rowboat out and go fishing. What about it, Bess?"

"You haven't caught a thing out there in thirty years, but yes, it's a beautiful day and some time out on the water would be wonderful!"

CHAPTER EIGHTEEN

"How much higher do we go?" Chad hollered from below.

"About a half a mile or so," Pete yelled back, raising his voice above the sound of the waterfall. "We should be there before lunch!"

They were climbing a twisting path that wove its way through the dense foliage near the rushing water. Pete led the pack, having been to the old miner's cabin on a previous ride. Chad followed as close behind as he could, but his couch-potato life was catching up with him. Even though Pete was twenty years older, he was in much better physical condition.

Janet caught up with them as they neared the top of a steep incline. "It's not much easier going down," she puffed as she pulled herself up beside Chad. "Pete found this place about a year ago when he was up here with another group. He told me all about it. I've heard some of the *old miner* legends, but never had a chance to come up." She stopped to listen. Pete was calling them from above and waving. "We'll be right there," she called back, waving to him.

The two stragglers emerged from the overgrown path to see a small log cabin on a grassy plateau overlooking the valley. The roof, while still intact, was sagging, the door hung ajar, and one corner of the structure had collapsed. Pete stood at the edge of the path, allowing

Chad and Janet to get the full impact of the scene. After a moment he said, "What do think? Worth the climb?"

"Wow! What a sight!" Janet exclaimed. "You can see the whole valley from here!"

"And look!" Chad was pointing across the valley. "Way over there is the Lodge. Maybe they're looking at us with binoculars! I'll wave just in case." He began jumping up and down waving his arms. "Hi Mom! Hi Mom!" he hollered. "Look up here! I made it!" He ran over to the cabin. "Can we go inside?"

"Let's wait till after lunch," Pete suggested. "Before we go inside, I'd like to tell you about the man who lived here. That way, you'll have an idea of what he was like and his cabin will mean more to you. Okay?"

Chad nodded. "Sure." He was anxious to explore, but the past few days had taught him to think before he acted, and he sensed that Pete wasn't just putting him off.

Each of them had carried rations with them on the hike, and sat on an outcropping, snacking and dangling their feet over the edge. Janet pointed out the pristine quality of the area and the way the rock was layered. Chad had developed an interest in geology, although limited because of living in the city. He was fascinated by Janet's knowledge—she even knew the history of the nearby mountains and could identified features of the area that attracted prospectors, including the old miner who built the cabin.

"Many years ago, even before the Lodge was built down near the lake, there were rumors that gold had been found in the stream below the waterfall." Peter began. "Many men—even a few women—rushed to this area to pan for flakes of gold in the gravel bars of the stream. Very few of them found any gold, but some prospectors eked out a few dollars, and that attracted ruthless men to the site.

"One such man was Black Jack Callahan. He was a huge fellow, and before long he had fought everyone in camp and beaten them. He was a real scoundrel, and through cheating, trickery and outright intimidation, he gained control over almost every claim on the riverbank.

But there was one man who would not be scared off. Black Jack tried everything. He smashed his chute, ran off his mule, diverted water to flood his claim—he used every trick he could think of to get him to leave. No such luck. The prospector stayed, and became one of the most successful placer miners that had ever worked a claim. Every day he seemed to know exactly where the gold was, and by sundown he always had a bag full of gold dust that he hid somewhere during the night.

"So one evening Black Jack stayed awake to see what was going on. About midnight he saw the man emerge from his tent and go into the forest. Jack followed him. There he watched as a raven flew down from a tree, strutted around and had a conversation with the man. Jack wasn't close enough to hear what the raven said, but he saw the man take some food from his pack and give it to the bird. The next day Jack watched as the man went directly to a particular place along the stream, put his pan in the gravel, swirled it around, and poured a good measure of gold into his pouch. That night, the scene was repeated. The raven talked to the man and the man gave it some food."

Pete paused for a sip of water. "*Aha!* Jack thought, *the raven is telling the man where to find the gold and the man is rewarding the bird by giving it food!* When morning came, he was ready. He hit the prospector over the head with a stick and tied him up. That night, it was Black Jack himself who went to meet the raven.

"'He's gone home' Black Jack said to the raven. 'He has sold me his claim and I am to speak with you and you will tell me where the gold is.' But the raven was wise, and didn't believe him. So he told Callahan that all the gold had been found, and there was no more in the creek. Callahan grabbed the bird and started to choke it. 'Liar!' He screamed. 'Show me the gold or I will destroy you!' 'Alright,' the bird whispered 'I will tell you'. Jack released his hold a little. 'The only gold is high above the falls. You must climb there and mine it from the rock itself.'

"The man thought this was logical, as the gold would have washed down from higher in the mountains, so he released the bird. 'Now I need food for my children' said the bird. 'That is my reward.' But Black Jack Callahan now knew where the gold was, so he refused to give the raven any payment for the information.

"Callahan climbed up to this meadow, using all his strength to haul up his equipment and supplies. He built that cabin over there," Pete said, pointed toward the old building, "and set about the task of discovering the motherlode from which the flecks of gold washed down into the stream. He worked all summer and fall, but could not find the vein of gold. Winter set in, and he still searched. He became sick, but still his search did not end. In spite of the bitter cold, he went back to the rock daily, looking for the fortune, but could not find it.

"One day a little mouse came to him. 'If you give me wool so I may make a nest for my children, I will tell you where the treasure lies,' the mouse said. 'Agreed,' said Callahan. 'The treasure lies within' the mouse responded. 'All that you seek is buried inside. You will not find true wealth unless you look deep inside and cease to search the world for something that is within your grasp.'

"The miner pondered the saying of the little mouse, but refused to grant her the wool for her nest. 'I know where the gold is!' he exclaimed. 'It's beneath the cabin'. And so he tore up the floorboards and began digging. Alas, there was no gold. He refused to understand the true meaning of what the little mouse had said."

Pete stood and began walking toward the cabin. The other two joined him as he approached the door. "Why don't you go inside first?" he said to Chad.

Chad opened the door cautiously, not knowing what was hidden in the gloomy interior. When his eyes adjusted to the dim light, he looked around. There was an old table against one wall and a raised bedframe against the other. What shocked him though, was the big hole in the middle of the floor. The boards had been torn up and the dirt excavated all the way down to bedrock. "Wow! So it's true what you said. He did try to find the treasure inside the cabin!"

"Apparently he did try," responded Pete, smiling. "But he didn't understand that the true treasure lies within the heart."

"So what happened?" Chad asked, not sure whether Pete was kidding him.

"Well, no one ever knew what happened to Black Jack Callahan. Some say his ghost haunts these mountains as it goes on searching for the treasure. And legend has it that's why the raven always tries to steal food from a campsite. He has never been paid for telling the miner where the gold was. That is also why the little mouse takes bits of blanket, string or other soft cloth for its' nest."

"I'd like to take my dad up here. Do you think I could?" Chad asked. "I'd like to show him this cabin and tell him the story. Would it be possible?"

"Do you think you're ready to spend some time alone with your father?" Janet responded.

"I really think so," Chad answered thoughtfully. "I mean I've learned so much this past week and I'd like to share it with him. I don't know what's been happening back at the Lodge, but it really doesn't matter. I've made some changes and I think I can really be different with my folks now. Like the story you told, the true treasure is in the heart, and I believe I understand a lot more than I did before. I want to get to know my folks better—especially my dad."

"Well, we usually stay up here a little longer, but if that's what you feel inside, then I think we should head on back to the Lodge and ask your dad if he wants to spend some time with you. What do you think he'll say when you ask him?"

"I don't know. I really don't." Chad replied. "But I have to try."

CHAPTER NINETEEN

"THEY'RE HERE!" MIRIAM CAME RUSHING INTO THE Lodge, pointing over her shoulder toward the stables. "They're here!" She grabbed Ian's arm and pulled him toward the door.

"Who's here?" Ian asked as he was dragged away from his supper.

"Chad and Janet and Pete! They're back! I thought I heard something and then I saw them coming down the trail toward the barn." She turned and looked at Charlie. "I thought they weren't supposed to be back for a couple of days yet. I hope nothing's happened!" She stopped talking long enough to catch her breath. "Oh God, I hope nothing happened to Chad, I'd never forgive myself!" She gave up trying to pull Ian and ran up the trail toward the corral.

"Chad! Chad!" She yelled as she ran. She could see them dismounting and tying the horses to the fence. When Chad heard her voice he turned and ran toward her, meeting her part way down the trail and scooping her into his arms and swinging her around. "How come you guys are back early?" she asked as Chad set her down. "Did something happen?"

"Yes Mom, something happened!" Chad replied. "Something great! I can't wait to tell you about it! Oh, first I've got to give Shiloh a rubdown and give him some oats, and then I'll tell you. Okay?" He took his mother over to where the horses were tied.

Miriam watched, fascinated, as her son quickly stripped the horse of its tack and began the rubdown. He was so full of confidence! No signs of the surly, angry young man who'd left on the trail ride. His hair was plastered down from being jammed under the Stetson for so long, and he was dirty! "You need a bath!" she chided. "Didn't you wash when you were on the trail? You smell like a blend of horses and wood smoke!"

"I went for a swim!" he replied. "Not for very long—the water was too cold." He sniffed his shirt. "I guess I do stink. That's what I've been doing for six days—sitting over a campfire and riding a horse. And I am looking forward to a good shower and sleeping on a mattress again." He paused and looked around. "Where's Dad?"

"I think he's on his way up. We were just finishing supper when I heard the horses, so I ran up here to see if everything was okay."

Then Chad spotted his father standing by the corner of the barn looking at him. "Hi Dad. Where did you come from?"

"I got here just after your mom did, and watched you unsaddle your horse. You sure know what you're doing!" He walked over and put his arms around his son.

Chad chatted with his dad about the horse as he worked. He finished his routine by taking the hoof pick and cleaning out Shiloh's hooves. "Do you know what they call that?" he asked his father, pointing to a feature of the hoof.

"I don't know. A foot?" he replied.

"No, I mean the little pointed part, right here." He put his finger on a small protrusion in the middle of the hoof. "It's called a *frog*. Isn't that neat? I learned a whole bunch of new stuff."

Ian was seeing his son in a different light. "It looks like all of us have been getting an education. I don't know what else besides horsemanship you've been doing, but down here we've been going through a real learning curve. We've been talking about things that have really made me think."

Chad finished working on Shiloh's hooves and stood up. "I just want to say I love you, Dad. And thanks for putting up with me so long."

"I love you too, Son. Always have. Even though I didn't show it sometimes. I'm proud of you. I don't think I could have gone off to the hills like that." He stepped back, holding Chad at arm's length and looking him up and down. "You look good—lean and strong, but, like your mother said, you've developed quite a smell!" They both laughed.

"I've really learned a lot. Not just about horses and *the way of the trail*, but about me. We did a lot of neat stuff too." He turned as Pete came up and took Shiloh's halter rope out of Chad's hand.

"I'll put your horse away. You go visit with your folks. You got a lot to catch up on. Janet and I will stable the horses and grab a shower. You can tell Bess we'll be down for supper in an hour. Okay?"

Chad nodded. "Thanks Pete. I appreciate it." He turned to his folks. "Now, let's get down to the house. On the way I tell you about the trip. It was incredible!"

Chad walked proudly down the path with his parents, his arms linked in theirs—all of them wanting to share their experiences and hear the news.

Chad's story was all over the place. He would start one thought, then switch to another, telling his folks about a cougar he'd seen, then about making supper, then again about tracking a deer along a trail.

"What a story you have to tell!" Ian laughed, holding up his arms in surrender. "I think we've all had some pretty incredible things happen to us. I'm just so happy we came up here. And to think I just about left! I want to hear about *the way of the trail* and everything you've learned." He stopped and looked into Chad's eyes. "Son, in case you didn't hear me, I love you. Things have happened here that opened my eyes—and my heart. I'm sorry for what I put you and your mother through, but things have changed. No—I've changed. I want to spend time with you. Time that I wish I could reclaim from when I worked after hours, or from when I just didn't have my priorities straight."

"I'd like that too Dad," Chad said quietly. "I haven't been the greatest son in the world either, but at least now we get a second chance. There are lots of families that never find out there's a better way. I'll never be able to thank Judge Stevenson enough for ordering me up here."

"Neither will I, Chad. Neither will I. I have to tell you though, when you left the house without breakfast that day, and I found out you'd be up in the hills for two weeks, I decided to go back to town. Fortunately, Charlie talked me into taking a walk with him. I didn't want to go, but after spending a morning with him, I didn't want to leave."

"I know what you mean Dad. When I took Pete's truck and went back to the city I had made up my mind never to come back. In fact, I had decided to run away all together." As they approached the little spring that cut through the trail he stopped. "I want to tell you what happened."

"You don't have to Chad," his mother said, stopping beside him. "It's enough that you decided to come back."

"No Mom, it's not enough. I know we're not a very religious family, but I really believe God was watching over me that night." He relayed the story of his wild drive into town. When he told them about the police and the robbery Trevor committed, they were shocked.

"So how come they let you go?" Miriam asked, and listened in amazement to Chad describe the incident with the semi-trailer.

Ian put his arm around his son. "You're right, we haven't been a very religious family. But I think everything that's happened to us lately has been a series of little miracles. Maybe, when I think about it, they weren't so little. I mean, look at us standing here. Could you imagine this a week ago?" They all chuckled. "I believe that God has something special planned for this family of ours. I don't know what and I don't know when. But I do feel that if we leave the future in His hands and just do what we know is right, then sometime we'll be able to help someone else."

They continued walking to the lodge. "I wish we didn't have to go home right away." Chad said, looking at his parents.

"Neither do we," his mother answered. "It's wonderful to have you back, but I was looking forward to spending some more time with Bess and Charlie. I guess now that the ride is finished we'll be heading back to town."

"Dad," Chad began tentatively, "I have something to ask you." He waited for Ian to look at him. "When we were up in the mountains, I asked Pete if I could take you on a short ride back up to a place where we camped." Chad didn't wait for a response. "Janet calls it a *guiding ride*. That's because I've been there and can take someone else along the same path I went. You can even ride Shiloh—he's a great horse. And I'll take Pete's mare. I already asked him and he said yes. So, what about it? Can we do it?"

"I haven't been on a horse since I was your age," Ian replied. "I don't know if I even know how to get on one, let alone ride along those narrow paths up there. Maybe if we just stick to some of the lower trails, we can go out for an afternoon." He could sense the disappointment in his son.

"If we just stick to the easy trails, Dad, we won't see anything! You can do it. Before I went on the trail with Pete and Janet, I had only ridden once, and this time we'll go a lot easier. We can take our time and visit along the way. Please?"

"Oh, okay. You talked me into it. If it's okay with Mom?" He turned to Miriam. "Were you serious about wanting to spend a day or so with Bess and Charlie?"

"I think it would be wonderful for you two," she answered. "Yes, I'd love to spend some more time here at the Lodge, and you and Chad can catch up on things. I think it's a great idea."

Ian gave in, laughing. "Okay," he said, "but you'll have to go easy on me. Just remember, I'm not a very good rider, so none of this galloping or racing. Agreed?"

"Agreed." Chad held out his hand and father and son shook on it. "And, just for your information, you never gallop trail horses unless it's an emergency. Too many chances of injuring the horse, so I won't go faster than a trot, and then only when the trails are wide open. Besides, we'll be packing rations and bedrolls so we have to watch we don't lose anything."

CHAPTER TWENTY

THE GROUP ARRIVED AT THE FRONT STEPS OF THE Lodge, where Charlie and Bess greeted them. "Welcome home Chad!" Bess exclaimed, giving him a grandmotherly hug and a big kiss on the cheek. "Did you have a good time?"

"I had a wonderful time. And guess what? Dad's going out on the trail with me! Isn't that cool?"

"That is cool." Bess replied, turning to her husband. "Isn't that wonderful Charlie?"

"It sure is. Where are you planning on going, Chad?"

"We'll camp at the waterfalls and then hike up to the old miner's cabin, so I can show Dad around!"

"Ah, Black Jack Callahan's place eh? I remember the first time Bess and I hiked up there. We were a bit younger of course, but it's a great place to camp. And the stories about the cabin—what did you think?"

"I loved them! Pete told me some and so did Janet, but don't tell Dad! I want to do the same thing so he can see the place after I tell him about the Raven and the Mouse."

"Of course we won't! In fact, we never tell the stories unless we're up there. You just can't get in the right mood sitting down here sipping hot chocolate with your slippers on." Charlie turned to Ian. "So when is this adventure of yours and Chad's start?"

"I'm not sure." He turned to his son. "When are we heading out?"

"Well, I'd like to get going by about noon, the day after tomorrow. That way we can camp at the same spot Janet, Pete and I did the first night we were on the trail. I know the way and we can get there if we leave early enough. We have to get our stuff together and pack the horses. I think the mounts need a day off before going back out, and besides, I kind of want to sleep in a bit tomorrow. So if it's okay with you, we can head out about lunch time, the day after tomorrow?"

Ian nodded. "That's alright with me. I think the first day should be a bit short so I can get used to riding again. When would we be coming back?"

"If we take the route we took on our way back, we can be up there on the second day, and then come back. That'll be four nights on the trail. Two up and two back." He grinned at his father. "Unless you're too old and out of shape to make the trip, that is."

Ian took a good-natured jab at his son. "I'll show you who's out of shape. I'll have you know I grew up tough! We didn't have any of these fancy conveniences your generation has. We had to make do with what we had!"

Chad rolled his eyes and looked at Charlie. "Oh now he's going to tell everyone how he had to walk to school, uphill, through the blowing snow wearing his father's socks on his hands, and how one winter all they had to eat was 50 pounds of buckwheat!"

The adults laughed. "Just you wait, young man. When you have kids you'll be telling them how you had to ride a wild horse up the side of a mountain, being chased by a bear and how you had to climb a tree and rob a bee hive to toss honey at the bear to get him to leave you alone! I can't wait to hear how the myths surrounding this trip will grow when you're as *old and out of shape* as I am!"

"Myths! Did I hear someone say adventures on the trail are myths"? Pete's booming voice echoed through the room. "I'll have you know that it wasn't just any wild horse Chad had to ride up the side of the mountain, it was the wildest horse that was ever known! And it wasn't just up the side of the mountain, but over the top, up a glacier and through a cave—without a saddle! And the bear? That was *Old Three Toes*, the meanest grizzly in these parts. The bees were African Killer Bees, and after Chad threw down the honey to the old bear he lassoed the largest bee in the hive, saddled it and rode it to a standstill! Those aren't just stories, folks, they're legends!" By this time everyone was roaring at Pete's playful narration.

Janet pulled a chair up to the table and joined the group. "My nose tells me that you have been so busy talking you haven't had a shower." She wrinkled her nose. "Here Pete and I put the horses away, showered, changed and came down for supper, and you haven't even started. You're so busy telling tall tales!"

"Sorry about that folks," Chad said, pushing back his seat and standing. "I'll be back in a couple of minutes. Bess," he asked his hostess, "would it be possible to get some supper after I shower? I'm starved."

"Of course, Chad. You get washed up, and when you come down I'll have some food for the three of you. Now scoot upstairs before Janet gets real cranky."

Chad headed for the stairs and was watched as he bounded up to his room.

"I would never have believed this a week ago," Ian said, nodding toward the stairs. "He's so relaxed and happy. Something has really changed for him." He turned to look at Pete and Janet. "I don't know and I won't ask what happened up on the trail, but I do want to thank you from the bottom of my heart for giving us our son back."

Miriam was nodding in agreement. "When you folks came back early I was afraid something had happened to him. Something did, but it certainly wasn't something I needed to be worried about. Like Ian said, thank you for what you've done."

"Chad isn't the only one who's changed," Janet said. "The way you two greeted him when he came back and the warmth and love you showed, tells me that change happened back here at the old ranch too!" She nodded toward Ian and Miriam. "Change begins in the heart—that's the foundation—but that's not where it ends. To really create lasting change, the family itself has to build on that foundation. If I know Bess and Charlie, you've been talking about the individual doing the right thing, and then working together as a couple. Am I right?"

The Jamison's nodded.

"After supper, I'd like to lead a discussion on family. It made a huge difference in our life, and although we don't have children, we have to operate both as a couple and as a family." She paused. "I know you've been married longer than Pete and I. But we work with the young people who come here, and Bess and Charlie get to spend time with the parents. So it's always a treat for us when we can meet the parents and share some of our experiences. It's not so much our helping them, as them helping us. We get a lot out of these sessions and it helps us as much as we hope it helps you. Would you folks be okay with that?" Ian and Miriam were nodding in agreement. "This isn't going to be a session where we all throw our hurts and angers on the table, but more the sharing of ideas about families and how each of us can strengthen and encourage each other." She continued until she saw Chad coming down the stairs.

As Janet spoke, Bess had been busily setting the table for the trail riders. When Chad reclaimed his chair and sat up to the table, she served the food. As was the custom at mealtime in the Lodge, they bowed their heads and gave a prayer of thanks for the food. Conversation ceased as the hungry riders enjoyed the change from trail fare to a meal from Bess's kitchen.

CHAPTER TWENTY-ONE

"WHERE DO YOU WANT US TO SIT?" CHARLIE ASKED Janet as he and Chad cleaned up after supper.

"Wherever Janet wants us to sit I hope it's on something soft," Chad chimed in. "My butt is still sore!"

"Why don't we stay inside?" Janet replied. "That way Chad can have one of the soft chairs and we can all enjoy the fire." She walked over to the fireplace, and arranged the furniture in a circle. "Just sit wherever you want," she announced, waving her hand toward the assembled chairs. "This is informal—just a sharing of things that have made a difference in other families and hearing your experiences."

Pete led the way. "Janet and I feel very strongly about the whole concept of family. As Janet said, we spend more time with kids than parents. I think it's important that you have an idea of where we're coming from and why we feel so strongly about family."

Pete told the story of his youth. Although Bess and Charlie had heard it before, they were still fascinated. He told of how his mother had run off with another man and left his father with an infant to raise. He recounted the passing of his father and the years spent being shuffled from one foster home to another, never having roots or the feeling of belonging to a family.

"And finally, at thirteen, I ran away for good. I hit the streets, surviving any way I could. I was lucky, in that a veteran cop found me sleeping in a vacant warehouse. He knew about the Lodge up here at Lake Sandoza and brought me to stay with Charlie and Bess. I started working with the horses, helping another couple with the trail rides, and I've been here ever since. This is my home, and these folks," he pointed to Bess and Charlie, "I've adopted as my family."

"My story is different, but there are parallels." Janet said as she began her tale. "In my case it was my Dad that ran off. He divorced my Mom and, let me tell you, it was tough growing up in a single parent home. I became really wild when I was about fifteen or so, and with no father in my life I didn't know how to act around men. I thought my value was in my looks and my body and I was always looking for attention from men. That got me into all sorts of trouble. One time I stayed away from home for an entire weekend and on Monday I was called into the guidance counselor's office. My mother was there, as was the principal and the counselor. Mrs. Tarkowski was her name and, like the police officer who picked up Pete, and the judge who dealt with you, Chad, she knew about this place. She sent both Mom and I up here when I was seventeen." She paused, looking lovingly at Pete.

"At the time Pete was almost twenty-one—an older man by my reckoning. And at first I used all my wiles to get him to do the things I wanted from him. I flirted, I pouted, and I flattered. I even brought out the heavy artillery and tried to seduce him. But he was immune to everything I tried. I didn't think he even noticed me, and then when I realized he noticed me but wasn't interested, I figured something was wrong with him!

"It wasn't until I came back up here a few years later to take a break from university that I realized that he cared a lot for me. Earlier, he just didn't want to get involved with a silly seventeen-year-old! The rest, as they say, is history. We fell in love and when I finished college we got married." Janet allowed her husband to continue the story.

"When we decided to marry, we spent a lot of time talking about family. Both of us had come from destructive homes and knew that if we wanted a solid marriage and a solid family, we were going to have to change the pattern set by our parents. We had chosen to become a family, and we entered into that decision with our hearts open and receptive, both to each other as individuals and to us as the nucleus of a family."

"We were at a disadvantage compared to some other couples, yet we had an advantage over many," Janet continued. "The disadvantage was that we had very little history to build on. The advantage was that with such little background, we weren't chained to the past like many of our peers. We could start fresh."

"How do you mean *start fresh*?" Miriam inquired.

"What we did was make a very conscious decision to create for ourselves a family history. Are all your grandparents still living?" She looked at Chad and he nodded. "Your family has a history. Both sets of grandparents are still alive, your parents have not separated or divorced, and I would imagine there are aunts and uncles on both sides of the family as well as cousins, etc. Is that correct?" Chad nodded again.

"Well, *we* didn't have that. Outside of my mother, we have no relatives that we are aware of. So, in a way, we had almost no roots to anchor us." She paused to think.

"Well, don't stop there," Chad urged. He turned to his parents. "We talked a lot on the trail, and I think what they did is really neat. I'd like us to do it—maybe when we get back. What do you think?"

Ian smiled. "I haven't heard what they did. After Pete and Janet tell us how they built their family roots, maybe we can clone it for ourselves."

Chad nodded and turned around again. "Okay, Janet, sorry for interrupting."

Janet walked over and stood in front of the fireplace. "Many times, families just come together without much thought. That's understandable. But what is tragic is that they continue through life without thinking about their family as a unit. We hear about the *family unit* but we seldom give the phrase much thought." She picked up the old weathervane from the mantle. "Let me illustrate. Like this old piece of tin that sat atop the barn for decades, many families just park themselves in a comfortable spot and let the wind point the direction they should go. Whether it's jobs, schooling, social activities, their spiritual life, volunteering—whatever—they don't take time to examine where they came from or where they're going.

"When Pete and I got together, one of the first things he said to me was 'Janet, we're a family. I know from my experience that a loving family is special. But we need to know *where we were*, so we know *where we are* and can plan *where we'll go*.' So we spent a lot of time on what we call *The Family Business*."

Pete walked over and stood beside his wife. "It's been a wonderful experience for us, and we'd like to share some ideas that we're incorporated into our family business. Maybe you can use some, and we'd also like to hear some of your ideas that we could integrate with ours. After all," he smiled at Janet, "we plan on having children some day, and need all the information we can get!"

"We would love to hear about your *Family Business*," Miriam said. "It's such a treat for us to spend time with both you folks and with Charlie and Bess. You're just starting out on your life together, and these wonderful people," she looked at the older couple, "have been together for more than four decades! I think we can gain a lot from both of you!"

"The first thing we had to do was decide on a last name." Janet began. "I know, it sounds like a simple thing, right? Well it wasn't. Traditionally, the woman takes the man's last name. Oh, I know that some women keep their last names, or maybe hyphenate their last names, but we wanted to decide for ourselves what family name we would use. And we wanted both of us to have the same last name. We were determined to be a family unit, remember?" She smiled at Pete.

"Well, we discussed it at length. And I do mean at length!" Pete chuckled. "When we finally made the decision, it was actually *my* last name we decided on. Not because it was short, or rhymes with anything, but because it was the only thing I had from my past. So Janet agreed to take my name—Balinich. Once that was decided, we then wanted to establish our own identity."

It was Janet's turn again. "First, we needed to know the history of the name Balinich. What was unique about it? Where did it come from? It sounds like it may have originated in Central Europe. But which country? The Balkans, or further north? We dug up everything we could find. We also did some research on historical figures named Balinich. We wanted to know if there were any famous people in the family tree—or any that had been hung as horse thieves! But we couldn't find any references at all!"

"You may be surprised to hear that over 83% of the public do not know the origin of their name or any significant history of their family. That included us! Then we did a search of our given names. I was named after a great aunt, but we couldn't find any information about Pete's name. So, we decided that, as there were some great men named Peter—Peter the Great, The Apostle Peter—we would assume the best: that he was named for a great leader.

"There wasn't a Balinich coat of arms, so we decided that we needed our own unique adaptation of our history. Take a look at the wall over here." Janet moved to the wall and pointed out a number of shields and crests. Identifying a particular one as theirs, she continued. "When you get a chance, take a look at it. We incorporated a special badge and motto. But in addition, we added the date we met and the date we were married. We also included," she pointed again at the shield, "the figure of a horse signifying our love of the animal, and a pine cone to show our respect for the forests."

"That's beautiful," Ian exclaimed. "It's something we'll be working on as soon as we get home. I love it! To have your very own coast of arms—that you created. Not just something from generations past, but right now—for your own family!" He walked over for a closer look. "You guys sure put a lot of thought into the design. What's this for?" He asked pointing to a blank square of metal on the plaque.

"That's where we'll add the names and dates of birth of our children when we have them," Pete answered. "We want the family crest to be a current memorial. As milestone events happen to us or to our children, we'll add them to the shield, keeping a visual record of our family history."

"Most of society celebrates the arrival of each new year," Janet continued. "For us, each December 31st is a time to look back with thankfulness at the past year. We talk about what's happened and how it affected us as individuals and as a family. We take down the family shield and reminisce about the events recorded on the shield. Eventually we'll add more information, but we've decided that we'll include only the major events."

"Now it's your turn." Charlie said, speaking to Ian. "What advice can you share to make a *Family Business* run better?"

"Well," Ian began, "as you know, my background is in business, and I think some aspects of a family can be run on a business-like basis. Reading some books on business management might be a good place to start."

Pete interrupted him. "Ian, I wasn't talking about operating our family on a business-like basis. I know that's your background, but I don't think a family can function in the same manner as a profit-based company."

"Let's think about that for a moment." Ian replied. "If a business is to be profitable, there has to be goals, objectives, functions, tasks and, ultimately, a CEO who makes the final decisions. If families operated on that basis, I think there would be fewer problems."

"Whoa there. Just a minute," Janet jumped in. "Are you suggesting that to be successful a family has to be structured like an organization chart? I couldn't disagree more! A business operates to make a profit and often shows little concern for its employees and even less for the environment or their customers. I know! I've lived in the city and I've worked for large corporations!"

Ian held up his hand, signaling Janet to stop. "Look, I'm not saying they're exactly the same, but I think there are some parallels. I mean, didn't you call your process a *Family Business*? "

"Yes, we do call it a *business*, but not in the way *you* mean business!" Janet said, looking a little defensive.

"This is a great discussion," Charlie joined in, "and I think we should pursue it. But not right now. Everyone's tired—it's been a long day. How about tomorrow morning after breakfast? Is everyone okay with that?"

After some good-natured grumbling, it was agreed to postpone the debate until the next morning.

Then Charlie added, "Before we head off to bed, I'd like to offer one thought to sleep on. I think both of you," indicating Janet and Ian, "have excellent points and I'm looking forward to tomorrow. May I suggest that there are at least two ways the word *business* can be defined. The first is the way Ian sees it—as a commercial or industrial enterprise for profit. The second is the way Janet and Pete see it—as a serious activity requiring time and effort, without distractions, as in *getting down to business*. Am I correct in what I am hearing?"

The debaters nodded in agreement with Charlie's summation.

"Well then," Bess said, wanting to close on a friendly note. "We could probably go all night, but I think Chad is about ready to fall asleep sitting in his chair. If everyone agrees, we'll adjourn until tomorrow after breakfast," she said, smiling at each one in turn.

Miriam leaned over and touched Chad. He straightened quickly, pretending he hadn't been dozing. "We're all going to bed now. It's been a big day for you—and for us! I'd also like to hear more about your adventures. Okay?" He nodded sleepily.

Everyone stood and said their goodnights. Ian, Miriam and Chad went upstairs and Pete and Janet took their leave, heading up the trail to their place.

As the house grew quieter, Bess leaned over and gave her husband a peck on the cheek. "You're a bit of a devil aren't you? You knew you could get a heated discussion going, knowing Ian's background in business, and how Pete and Janet feel about big business!" She chuckled. "I love these discussions, and I'm really looking forward to seeing how it plays out tomorrow. Are you?"

"Of course I am," Charlie said, taking her arm. "We'll see if anyone changes their mind, or if there's some sort of compromise. That's what our role is, isn't it? To have people examine their beliefs and apply some of the principles they already know." They carried the coffee mugs to the sink, leaving them for the morning. After turning off the lights they, too, headed off to bed.

Upstairs, Miriam turned to Ian as she prepared for bed. "I think this last week has been good for all of us. But I really am impressed by the changes in Chad. He seems so much happier now—and grown up! I couldn't believe it when I saw him with the horses!"

"I agree," Ian replied. "I just hope it lasts. There have been a couple of times over the years when we thought things would work out, but they never did." He held up his hand. "I'm not saying he isn't happy, but I am wondering if it will last. Maybe I'm just a pessimist, but I want to see some real change—long term—before I'm as convinced as you are."

"Well, maybe going up into the mountains with him will give you a chance to see if the change is real." Miriam was ready for bed. As she slipped under the comforter she added, "Give him a chance, will you Ian?"

He nodded in agreement and pulled back the covers on his own side of the bed. They lay awake for a while, not speaking, each of them deep in thought. As the house quieted, Miriam drifted off to sleep. However, Ian's mind was abuzz.

CHAPTER TWENTY-TWO

ALTHOUGH EVERYONE HAD SAID THEY WERE TIRED, the kitchen was bustling with activity shortly after sun-up. Ian had poured his second cup of coffee for the day and was seated at the table, a pile of papers in front of him. As the others sat down, he pushed the documents aside.

"I've been thinking about our conversation and the two definitions that Charlie gave before we went to bed, and I agree. There are two ways of thinking about *Family Business*, but I think they're compatible—they just have different goals."

"Hold on," Bess interrupted. "Let's have breakfast and keep the discussion for after. No one ever thinks first-class thoughts on a second-class stomach." Then she passed the heaping plates and poured glasses of juice as the group wolfed down their first meal of the day.

When the table had been cleared, Charlie looked around and decided it was time to open the discussion. "Okay, Ian, you were up half the night thinking about this. Why don't you get things rolling?"

"All right, let's approach this with a combined definition. That is, *Family Business* is a focused endeavor, but it should also incorporate economic purposes. Can we agree on that—at least for now?" He looked at Janet and Pete, who nodded.

"One of the fundamentals of any business is to have a mission statement, so the business will focus on what is important to it, and not go off-track all the time. I think this could also work for a family.

"Consider what Pete and Janet said last night about reclaiming their history. That's important. But there should also be a purpose for the family. I'd like everyone to pitch in and we can discuss a mission statement for our family. That's what we do in business. Every stakeholder, or person who has an interest in the company, states what they think is important to the organization, and then it is circulated, discussed and ultimately voted on by the shareholders. In this situation, with you folks," he indicated Pete, Janet, Charlie and Bess, "being so instrumental in rebuilding our family, could you help us?" All voiced their agreement.

"But ultimately, the mission statement must be decided by the three of you," Bess added. "After all, it's the three Jamisons who are the shareholders. Right?"

After some discussion as to how to proceed, Charlie left the room, returning shortly with a large pad of paper on an easel. "There. Now when someone has an idea we can jot it down. Then you folks can think about it and decide which, if any, fit your family. My writing isn't so good, so maybe Bess could be the scribe?" She readily agreed.

The morning passed as the group held a spirited discussion about the mission of families in general and of the Jamisons in particular. The antique schoolhouse clock on the wall showed almost noon when Bess called a halt.

"Okay, we have three possibilities," she announced. "Here they are: The first one focuses on the family itself, and it grew out of some of the discussion during the week." Bess read the mission statement to the group.

> *"The mission of this family is to allow each person to grow spiritually, physically, emotionally, and educationally to their*

maximum potential. Each member pledges to aid all other members in achieving their goals and ambitions.

"The second one still focuses on the family, but adds a bit of a *worldview* to the mission. Chad was the one who brought up the aspect of other people, and how the family can impact others." She recited the second statement.

"The mission of our family is to create an atmosphere of love, understanding, tolerance and respect amongst all members, and to present a unified front to the world. We will use our combined skills, assets and talents for the betterment of all.

"Now the third one kind of combines both the first and the second, but gets a little more specific about helping and respecting others. It builds on Chad's thoughts about other people."

"The mission of the Jamison Family is to care for our family by providing for each one's physical, emotional and spiritual needs. We will also care for our community, our city and our country. We respect all persons."

Then Bess concluded the presentation. "Those are three very powerful statements, but as I said earlier, the ultimate decision is not for the group, but for the shareholders. In this case, it's the three of you."

"Maybe we could adapt the ones you don't use," Pete said. "Now I want to thank all of you, and particularly Ian for giving us something very special to add to our *Family Business*." He addressed the group. "I'd like to suggest that we continue this afternoon if you're all willing?" Everyone was in agreement.

"Before we wrap up," Bess concluded, "and while we're still on the topic of business, maybe we can jot down a couple of topics so we don't lose our train of thought?" Bess, had participated in these exercises before and knew how easy it was for the process to lose its momentum.

"Ian, you're our business person. What other characteristics would a good business have?" Janet asked. "Will you write down the ideas as they come up?" Janet handed him the felt pen.

"All right. To be successful, a business has to develop a number of characteristics which help to keep it concentrated on the mission, and ensure that the business does its very best to achieve its goals. What characteristics would you suggest?"

Because Miriam was also in the business world, and had participated in a number of industry-related seminars, she was the main contributor to the brainstorming. Within half an hour, they had generated a list of topics to be discussed later in the day.

Ian printed each topic, and added an explanatory line beside each one.

Code of Ethics – *How the family conducts itself*

Public Relations – *How the family wants to be viewed in the community*

Job Descriptions – *The roles and responsibilities for each member*

Finance & Administration – *What the family earns and spends*

Goals and Objectives– *What the family does in the future: when and how*

"Look people," Ian said to the group. "We could, and probably will, add a few more topics. But, we've been sitting since breakfast. How about we call a halt, take a walk, and get back together after lunch? Even spending the three hours or so has given me a whole new appreciation of what a family can do for itself. I'd like to suggest that maybe Miriam, Chad and I take a picnic lunch, and talk about these things ourselves?"

"I agree on all fronts Ian," Pete responded. "Just sitting here has put my mind in overload. I think Janet and I would like some time to mull over these new ideas, but maybe I'd like to make one more suggestion." The group waited.

"What I would like to suggest is that Charlie and Bess be available to help each family if needed? I don't mean that they have to be with each family, but they've been at this a few years longer than any of us, and I think they can add some wisdom to the discussions. Agreed?"

"Agreed!" they said in unison.

They rose from the table and began preparing food they could take with them on their walk.

"So what do you think?" Charlie asked Bess as the younger folks left the Lodge.

"Well, I think this has been great for both the Jamisons and for Pete and Janet. I like the way Ian thinks. He has a great way of explaining things, and Miriam has a gentleness about her that brings out the best in the discussions. I think we might have a winning team here!" Taking their own lunch onto the porch, the elderly couple watched as the others disappeared into the trees.

Throughout the afternoon, the older couple had the wonderful experience of moving back and forth between the two families. Not once did they offer advice, but their interested questions and observations stimulated productive conversations amongst the parties.

By suppertime, the three Jamisons, as well as Pete and Janet, had made notes covering a wide range of family-business ideas, and more than once somebody was *volunteered* to go back to the Lodge for more writing paper.

As they gathered around the table for the evening meal, Miriam was the first to mention the events of the day. "I have to thank you, Janet and Pete," she said looking at each of them. "This has been an incredible experience. I'm actually looking forward to some time alone so I can get these notes," she lifted a bundle of papers, "into some sort of order."

During the evening there was time to review the day's activities, as the two families compared the results of their efforts. They shared freely their thoughts, concepts and beliefs. By bedtime they came to the realization that *Family Business* is much more than an economic unit, more than common goals and visions. It is a matter of the heart.

CHAPTER TWENTY-THREE

"CAN WE TAKE A BREAK?" IAN CALLED OUT. HIS SON was astride Pete's Appaloosa mare and riding twenty-five feet or so in front of his father. Chad turned to look back.

"What? You sore already? We've only been on the trail a couple of hours! Where's this *tough guy* you were telling me about?" He laughed as he pulled back on the reins, bringing his mount to a halt at the side of the trail. His father drew alongside.

"Hey, I'm still plenty tough! It's just that I thought this was to be a relaxing ride, not some Mounted Police marathon. And besides, I haven't had the training or experience you've had." He swung his right leg over the cantle, and lowered himself to the ground. After taking a few steps, he pushed his hands against his lower back and stretched. "I wish now I hadn't spent so much time behind a desk! This is killing me!" He looked up at his son, still in his saddle. "How much further do we go today?"

"Not too much further. A couple hours should do it, and then you can enjoy a good night's sleep lying on the ground!" he said, kidding his dad. "I know how you feel. The first day was a killer for me too, but don't worry—now that your muscles and backside are sore, tomorrow will be worse!" Chad hooked one leg over the saddle horn and sat crossways on the back of the horse. "Just walk a few minutes and you'll loosen up. The trail's smooth enough here, and we've actually made pretty good time. When we were up here a week or so ago there was three of us, and we went a little slower." He looked toward the sun. "We should be at the first campsite by mid-afternoon."

Ian took the reins and began to lead the horse. "Maybe I will walk a bit. It actually feels good to use my legs! It isn't just my back and butt that are sore, but trying to keep my toes pointed up instead of down is killing my calves. How come I can't just put my feet in the stirrups naturally?" he asked his son.

"It's simple Dad, really. You have to keep your heels down so that if the horse bolts or you get brushed off against a tree or something, your feet won't get hung up in the stirrup and drag you along the ground. I know it's a bit awkward at first, but once you get used to it, it's actually a lot easier on your legs. When you get back on, try squeezing your thighs against the horse. That'll take some of the weight off your lower legs as well as keeping your bouncing to a minimum."

After walking a half-mile or so, Ian remounted the horse and fell in behind Chad. "You're right," he said after a few minutes, "it does help if I squeeze my legs tighter into the saddle. But now I know why the old cowboys looked so bow-legged! This is tough!"

His son laughed. "Just hang in there. We're only about an hour or so from stopping, and you can relax for the evening." He pulled his horse alongside. "What happened to us, Dad? I mean, you and I used to do a lot of stuff together and then it just seemed to stop. I think this is the first time in the last three or four years that it's just you and me doing something with no one else around."

They stopped again, and Ian looked at his son. "I'm not really sure if there's any particular reason. I got busier and busier at work, you made friends and got involved at school, and we just stopped doing things together. I never realized how much things had changed until recently, and how much I missed spending time with you. When I finally appreciated what we once had, I thought I had lost it! I'm just so thankful for this time together. It's made me look at myself a lot closer and see what I've been doing—or not doing. It's been a rough week for all of us. I know I've had to do some soul-searching about who I really am and the kind of a person I've become, plus my failings as a husband and father."

Chad pulled back on the reins as the Appaloosa started to move. "I know what you mean. Being up here in the mountains has given me time to think about where I'm going and what kind of person I have to be to get there. It's been tough letting go of some of the baggage I was hauling around. It's given me a chance to look at things in a new way."

They started up again and moved along in comfortable silence for a while. The horses, surefooted and needing little guidance, carried their riders along the narrow trails, working higher and higher into the mountains. By mid-afternoon they had reached their destination and dismounted. Chad took charge, showing his father the camp routine of rubbing down the horses and ensuring they had the proper length of rope. They divided the chores between them, with Chad gathering the wood and lighting the campfire.

"I figured since we were planning on a relatively short trip today, we could afford the weight of bringing up a couple of steaks," Ian said, placing the meat in the pan. As it sizzled, he filled a saucepan with water and placed it at the edge of the fire to boil.

As the aroma of frying steak filled the air, Ian added rice to the boiling water. Within a few minutes the meal was ready and the two dug into their feast with enthusiasm. Chad had absconded with one of Bess's pies and cut it down the middle, giving his father half—more cherry pastry than Ian could remember eating at one sitting. "I don't know how you can lose weight eating like this," his father said, lifting up a forkful of pie. "This is something else!"

"Just wait till we hike up to the old miner's cabin tomorrow. You'll burn that off just getting to the first level." Chad gathered the utensils and began cleaning up.

They settled down for the evening, watching the fire burn and, for the first time in many years, enjoyed the evening, renewing their friendship and trust in one another. Occasionally one would stir from his comfortable position and add another log, then let it burn down to embers again.

"You know, Chad, what Charlie and Bess said affected me, but you know what really got me thinking? Even before I went up to their old place?"

Chad shook his head.

"It was Smudge! The day you took off in the truck, I went down to the lake. I was just so frustrated with everything! Smudge came over and tried to cheer me up. I gave him a cuff across the head." Chad looked at his father in surprise. "No, I didn't really hurt him—just his feelings. But it made me realize that I enjoyed feeling miserable! Regardless of what or who tried to help me, I was determined to be as miserable as I could. The dog didn't run away. He went to the edge of the dock and lay there—just looking at me. Eventually I gave him a petting, and he was so forgiving. He just excused my behavior and started our relationship off on a new foot."

"That's funny, Dad, because Smudge really made an impact on me too. It was the middle of the night when I got back, and I decided rather than wake everyone up, I would just sleep in the truck up by the stables. I wasn't sure whether or not I would be welcomed back, but I heard the dog outside the truck. I wasn't going to let him in, but I must have, because all of a sudden he was in the front seat with me. He was overjoyed to see me! I figured if he wanted me back, maybe that was a good start."

Eventually their conversation took a sleepy turn and, after saying goodnight, they wrapped themselves in their bedrolls and slept.

When morning arrived, the air had become noticeably cooler. At high altitude a late summer storm is not uncommon, and the wind blowing from the northeast carried a hint of a winter that was still months away. They rebuilt the fire, warming their hands over the flames as they waited for the coffee to boil. "Do you think we should go back?" Ian asked. "Those clouds look like a thunderstorm might be on its way."

"I don't think so, Dad. It's always cooler up here. I want to get up to the cabin today. We can be up there and back to the foot of the falls by nightfall and head back tomorrow. I don't think we'll get a storm. Maybe a bit of rain, but that shouldn't bother us too much."

Reluctantly, Ian agreed. He was enjoying the time with his son and seeing the changes that had taken place. He didn't really want to go back so soon. He was looking forward to the hike up to the miner's cabin and sharing the experience with his son. During their time together the previous evening, Chad was so enthused about the waterfall and was dying to tell him the legends of the area. Ian really didn't want to disappoint his son.

The weather cleared just after breakfast, and remained calm through the morning. They stopped for a cold lunch at noon, but the clouds gathered again, and the rain, which had held back during the early part of the day, began as a steady drizzle. They quickly remounted and continued their journey. By the time they had reached the foot of the cascade, the wind had pick up and they had to squint to see through the driving rain.

Moving under the shelter of the trees, they secured the horses and unrolled their groundsheets. Huddling beneath the protection of the rubberized material, they waited for the storm to let up. Chad yelled above the sound of the falls and the wind whipping through the trees. "We have to get the horses further into the bush!" He stuffed his protection under a dead log and moved toward the mounts. Ian did likewise and together they untied the horses to lead them to better protection.

They moved swiftly, trying to encourage the animals by tugging sharply on the halter rope. Chad's mare was confident in this hectic situation and followed willingly. Shiloh, however, had never experienced this severe a storm and was showing his insecurity. He balked at the unfamiliar urgency. As he reared back in opposition, several items fastened to the saddle began to loosen. First to fall was the saddlebag that had been tied to the saddle. Ian tried to grab it, but in doing so he caught the coil of rope that was looped around the horn. This half-inch sisal line was what they intended to use to stake the horses out on the lower meadow. As it unwound in his hand, the end of it flipped forward under the front feet of the terrified gelding. In his panicked state the young animal did not see a rope, he saw his worst horror—a snake!

Chad could only watch helplessly as his father was dragged back down the trail by the fleeing horse. He saw the frightened animal leap over a fallen log, ears back and nostrils flaring. As Shiloh lifted his front legs over the obstacle, he tore the rope from Ian's grasp and slammed him into the base of a tree. By this time Chad had secured his mount and was charging down the trail to where his father lay motionless.

As he slid and skidded along the path he yelled. "Dad! Dad! Are you okay?" He heard a low moan from his father. Chad knelt beside the injured man. "Dad, can you hear me?" Another moan.

Chad grabbed his father's wrist and felt for a pulse. There it was, strong and steady! *Maybe he's just had the wind knocked out of him* he thought. There was no sign of bleeding, but he didn't want to move his father for fear of aggravating any possible injury. He tore off the light jacket he was wearing and covered him, then scrambled back up the trail to get their groundsheets and recover the bedroll that had been shaken loose during Shiloh's mad dash.

When Chad returned with the gear, Ian had regained consciousness, but he was in obvious pain. "Sorry about that son," he gasped, as Chad bent down and tucked the bedding around him. "I tried to hang on, but when he jumped the log, he tore the shank rope out of my hand."

"It's my fault Dad," Chad replied, tears running down his cheeks. "I should have listened to you and turned back earlier. I'm sorry. Where does it hurt?"

"I hurt everywhere. I might have busted some ribs when I hit the tree. I don't think I can move."

Chad sat back, grinding the heel of his hand into his eyes out of frustration and anger at himself. "What are we going to do? Do you think we can double up on my horse?"

His father reached for his son's hand. "I don't think so, Chad. I can't move. I don't know what we can do outside of you going back to the Lodge for help."

"I can't leave you here!" Chad cried. "Maybe if I get you on the horse I can walk in front and we can get back that way."

"No Chad, that won't work. Just give me enough bedding to keep warm and go back to the Lodge and get help. I can't even stand, let alone sit on the back of a horse." The effort of speaking sent him into a fit of coughing and he cried out from the pain. When he wiped his hand across his mouth, there was a smear of blood on the back of his hand. "I must have punctured a lung," he wheezed. "Chad, you have to go back and get Pete. I'll be okay if I don't move around. Just tuck the bedrolls around me and head back." He paused to take a shallow breath, then squeezed his son's hand.

Chad nodded, not trusting himself to speak. Once again he scuttled back through the driving rain to where his horse was tied. He freed the halter shank and led the mare back down the path. He stripped his own bedroll from the back of his horse and tucked it snugly up under his father's chin. "I'll ride as quick as I can, but it'll be about twelve hours before I get to the lodge and then another twelve or so to get Pete back up here." He didn't know what else to say. He left the remaining food in a stack beside his dad, and mounted the horse. "I love you, Dad," he said. "I'll be back as quick as I can." He dug his heels into her flanks and was gone.

CHAPTER TWENTY-FOUR

"I hope the guys are all right," Pete said as he looked toward the mountains on the far side of the lake. "If they got up to the waterfall they're pretty well protected in the trees." He'd become worried when he saw clouds building up in the west and felt the temperature dropping.

"Is there anything we can do?" Janet asked. "I don't like them riding up there if a storm comes in. Maybe one of us should've gone with them."

"There's nothing we can down here except hope and pray. They should be all right though. Chad's been up there and back, and the horses are pretty familiar with the trail. We'll see how it is later before deciding what to do."

The couple had been working around the stable after spending the afternoon at the Lodge with Bess and Charlie and Miriam.

As they climbed the front steps Miriam and Bess met them. "How do you think they're doing up there?" Miriam asked, then looked toward the mountains.

"They should be okay. They have rain gear with them, and they can stay inside the miner's cabin where it's dry. They may be a half-day late getting back, but these late summer storms usually don't last long." Pete tried to sound reassuring.

"I'm just worried about them I guess." Miriam held the door as the others made their way into the house.

★ ★ ★

Darkness descended before Chad had gained the main trail back down the mountain. The poor visibility slowed his ride, and the muddy surfaces were tiring the horse. The mare, sensing the urgency of her young rider, was giving her all, but the demanding pace was rapidly sapping her energy.

Chad, sensed the exhaustion of the horse and eased up. In spite of his alarm over his father's injuries, he knew that if he was to get help in time, he needed the horse. There was no way he could walk the distance back to the Lodge in time to prevent his dad slipping into unconsciousness or developing pneumonia from the cold and wet. By midnight he reached the site where they had camped the first night. Barely giving it a glance, he pressed on, later pausing to allow the horse to drink at a stream.

★ ★ ★

Dawn had not yet arrived when Chad dismounted in front of the Lodge. Running inside he yelled. "Mom, Charlie, Bess! Dad's been hurt! Get up! We have to get help!"

Jarred awake by the shouting, first Miriam, followed shortly by the older couple, came scurrying down the stairs. "What happened Chad? What's happened to Dad?" She wrapped her arms around her shivering son, as he struggled to tell her the story.

Charlie, hearing the news, grabbed his coat and headed up the trail to rouse Pete and Janet.

Within ten minutes, the wrangler had pulled his truck in front of the Lodge. Charlie had brought him up to date on what happened, and both men entered the kitchen. Janet took the Appaloosa back up to the barn for a rubdown and some feed. The horse was near exhaustion and needed a vigorous massage to loosen its muscles. Janet also stripped the tack from the horse. It was wet, and after twelve hours of riding, friction burns would need tending.

"Chad, were exactly is your father?" Pete asked.

"Right beside the trail near the big meadow. You know, the one at the bottom of the falls?"

Pete nodded. "Okay. I'll drive down to the store and notify Search & Rescue. They have a chopper they use to get into the backcountry. From what you tell us Chad, your Dad isn't in any shape to ride out."

"Can I come with you?" Chad pleaded. "It's all my fault! Dad wanted to turn back when the storm started, but I made him go on!"

"Okay, come with me. You better change into something dry and warm; and Bess, could you make some hot chocolate or something? Chad's been riding for almost twelve hours in the rain and I'm real concerned. Maybe something to eat too?"

As Chad ran up the stairs, Bess headed into the kitchen to put the kettle on. Then she began fixing sandwiches for Chad to have on the road.

"Maybe he should stay here with us," Miriam suggested. "We could get him warm and dry and you could pick him up when you come back."

"That's really up to you and Chad. The rescue team will leave from their base and pick us up at the store. We won't be coming back here before we head up to get Ian."

Chad came bounding down the stairs just as Pete finished talking with Miriam.

"Mom. I'm going with Pete. I know where Dad is, and I want to go."

Miriam looked at her son. She saw the fear in his eyes that she may refuse permission, but also saw determination to participate in the rescue of his father. She nodded. "Okay, I think you should go. Just take care of yourself, okay?"

Chad slipped into a jacket that Charlie handed him, thanked Bess for the food and hot chocolate, and followed Pete out to the truck.

"Are you sure you're okay to go out again?" Pete asked, as they headed down the lane.

The young man nodded. "Yeah. I think Dad's hurt really bad. I...I didn't know what else to do! I had to leave him up there by himself!"

"I would have done the same thing, Chad. You had to ride out to get help—you didn't have much of an option. You did a very brave thing, riding all night through the rain. It was gutsy."

"But I was the cause of it all!" Chad repeated. "If we'd only turned back when Dad wanted, he wouldn't have gotten hurt."

"Well, that's not for me to make comment on. That's between you and your father. I wasn't there, so I don't know. Why don't we wait until we get him out, then you and he can talk about it? My gut tells me that your Dad will be proud of you for the way you've handled this situation."

Dawn was breaking as they pulled up in front of the country store. Pete banged on the door until the owner came to open it. After a brief conversation he motioned for Chad to join him. When Chad entered, the owner was already on the phone.

The merchant placed the receiver back on its holder. "I got hold of Jimmy Thurston, the paramedic just down the road, so they'll take off as soon as the bird's warmed up. I told him the two of you wanted to go along and he had no problems with that, so he should be here in fifteen minutes."

CHAPTER TWENTY-FIVE

EVEN THROUGH THE FOG OF EXCRUCIATING PAIN, IAN felt immense pride as he watched his son urge the horse to a gallop and vanish into the trees. In spite of the bedlam caused by the storm, Chad had reacted properly, keeping his wits about him and making critical decisions. Instinctively he had applied the knowledge he had gained through his association with Pete and Janet. Salvaging the bedrolls, taking proper precautions with the horses, and even ensuring his father was protected from the elements, showed a maturity and responsibility that had been absent just a few weeks earlier.

The injured man pulled the groundsheet tighter under his chin and, using his left hand, tried to tuck the edges of the wrap under his body. The entire area was soaking wet, and moisture had saturated his clothing from top to bottom. Ian knew if he didn't move to a more sheltered spot, he ran the very real risk of hypothermia. As his body temperature was bound to drop in the hours ahead, he needed to be as warm and dry as was possible.

He probed his right side carefully. He could feel the injury to his ribs and, taking care not to move quickly or to push beyond reasonable limits, he began to crawl. A rush of searing pain made him gasp, and he remained motionless for a moment, waiting for it to subside. When it regressed slightly, he continued his efforts, clenching his teeth to stifle an outcry. After what seemed like an hour or more he succeeded in crawling to slightly higher ground. But the driving rain still continued and the coverings he was using were waterlogged. Finally, he was able to pull himself up, turn around carefully, and sit with his back against a tree. After resting, he retrieved a nearby stick and used it as a sort of fishing pole to pull some bedding over his feet. There was little else he could do but hope that Chad could find his way back through the darkness and rain and bring help.

As the night passed, Ian gave in to uncontrollable shivering. He had read little on the subject of exposure, but what he remembered was that shivering was the body's way of trying to generate warmth. He also recalled that there would come a time when the shivering stopped, and this was a critical point in the downward spiral toward unconsciousness and finally death. He willed himself to stay awake and keep himself covered. He pulled part of the groundsheet over his head to minimize, as much as possible, the escape of body heat through his face and head. The sodden blankets provided little protection against the elements.

Through the darkness and rain, he struggled to remain conscious, knowing that to fall asleep could be fatal. A sliver of light broke the eastern horizon. The rain had ceased and the wind had died down. Ian did not see or hear these changes. His eyes had closed.

★ ★ ★

The whop-whop of the helicopter blades cutting through the high mountain air failed to waken the man lying alongside the trail. His only covering was a florescent yellow rescue blanket tucked tightly around him.

The pilot guided his craft carefully along the narrow valley, following Pete's directions. As they approached the meadow at the base of the falls, Chad pressed his face to the window, desperately seeking a glimpse of his father. While the rain had subsided, the moisture still lingering in the air made vision difficult. The craft settled gently onto the grassy area, and the occupants began disembarking. The paramedic handed his emergency kit to Pete, waiting outside the open door. Chad had jumped out as soon as the skids hit the ground and was running ahead of the others.

He quickly spotted the bright yellow rescue blanket. He rushed forward and knelt down beside his dad. "He's unconscious!" he yelled, looking back toward the chopper. "Hurry!"

Ian was oblivious to the sounds of the chopper and the voices around him. Even the shifting of his body onto the stretcher failed to pierce his unconscious state.

Chad was rubbing his father's hands, attempting to stimulate warmth. The medic gently restrained him. "We have to get his core temperature up. Don't rub his hands or feet. The blood in his extremities is cold, and if it starts moving, it can cause a heart attack. When we get him in the chopper, we'll put thermo-pad's around him and bring his temperature up gradually. Just keep talking to him. He's in bad shape but we haven't lost him yet!"

"What about giving him something to drink? I know he's unconscious, but can we get some hot liquid down to help him get warmer?" Chad was trying desperately to assist in some way.

"No we can't," the man answered. "He's unconscious, and we would risk the chance of choking him. And, even if we could, it would take about three gallons just to get his temperature up one degree. We'll get this wet clothing off, and wrap him in warm blankets. I think he'll make it, but we have to raise his body temperature gradually. Heating him up too quickly can be fatal."

The paramedic hadn't intended to offend Chad, but working in high stress situations had taught him not to worry about hurt feelings, just to focus on the needs of the patient. Chad could only assist by talking to his father and helping load him into the helicopter.

Once on-board, Chad and the medic stripped the wet clothing from Ian. Taking care not to aggravate the injured ribs, they wrapped the unconscious man first in an electric *body bag* and then rewrapped him in additional outer blankets. "We'll keep his head and face clear, and keep him as steady as possible as we lift off," the medic advised, as the pilot prepared the machine for flight. From the co-pilot's seat, Pete turned to watch the paramedic and Chad tend to Ian.

Within moments, the orange and red Eurocopter lifted from the meadow, banking as it rose. Their egress route followed the stream back through the foothills toward Lake Sandoza. Pete turned and motioned for Chad to lean forward.

"We're going to stop at the lodge so your mom can go with you and your dad to the hospital, okay?" Pete was shouting above the roar of the chopper.

"Is that safe though?" Chad replied. "Should we risk stopping?"

"It's right on our flight path, and it'll take only a minute or two. Your dad needs both of you, and I can't help any further. It's best if the family is together. Understand?" Chad nodded.

As the helicopter dropped toward the surface of the water and headed for a landing on the front lawn, the occupants could see four figures hurrying out from the Lodge. Janet had joined the other three awaiting word of the rescue.

The unit settled on the ground, and Pete was out the door and running as the rotors continued to beat the air. "Miriam," he yelled over the sound of the machine. "Get on board with Chad. They're taking Ian to the hospital in the city. You go with them and I'll stay here."

"How is he?" Miriam yelled back.

"Not too good. He's still unconscious. The paramedic is working to get his temperature up, but you have to get him to the hospital as soon as possible."

He took her by the arm and bent down as they passed under the whirling blades, then opened the door and helped her inside. The instant she was seated, the pilot lifted the machine into the air and headed for the city.

As the sound faded, Pete recounted the events of the rescue. "When we got to Ian he was in the last stages of hypothermia," he said as they climbed the steps of the Lodge. "I'm not sure about his ribs, but from what we can tell he's broken several, and it appears that his lung may have been punctured. He's in rough shape."

"How's Chad?" Janet asked. "He rode all night in the cold and wet."

"He seems to be okay, other than exhaustion. He's dry now, and warm, and I think it was good for him to go back up and get his father. He's a tough kid and pretty healthy. I asked the medic to have a doctor check him over when they get to the hospital."

Charlie poured a coffee for Pete. "What do you want us to do here?"

"If it's okay with you folks, I'll get Janet to run me down to the store in the Jamison's car so we can get the truck. It'll take an hour or so for them to get to emergency, then awhile before they can give us a report."

Janet turned to Charlie. "Can you keep an eye open for Shiloh? He'll probably make his own way back down. He might be a bit scatterbrained, but he does know where there's food and shelter. If he returns before I get back from the store, just put him in the stable." Charlie waved his agreement.

CHAPTER TWENTY-SIX

"IT'S MY FAULT, MOM," CHAD SOBBED AS THEY SAT together in the visitors' room awaiting word of Ian's condition. He described the accident, and how Shiloh bolted when the rope uncoiled like a snake. It was so clear in his memory—the horse panicking, his dad trying to control the animal, the mad dash along the trail and Ian being slammed into the trees... "And then he just lay there! I... I thought he was dead!" He put his head down.

Miriam embraced her son. "Chad," she said gently. "These past few days have been the happiest in many years for your dad. He was so proud of you, and so excited about going up into the hills with you. I know you feel guilty, but no matter what happens to Dad, just know that he wanted to be with you. I pray that he makes it okay but, regardless, he loves you very much."

The physical exhaustion and emotional roller coaster of the past twenty-four hours finally caught up with Chad. He stretched out on the green plastic-covered bench, laid his head on his mother's lap and, like he had done as a little boy, fell asleep. Miriam lovingly touched her son's hair as she said a silent prayer. *Oh God, please help Ian. We've just come together as a family and we need time to grow. Please don't take him now.*

The controlled chaos, apparent in all hospitals, was particularly difficult for Miriam. Her husband lay in serious condition in an examining room. She had remained with him as long as she could, but the medical staff had asked her to leave when the surgeon arrived to repair the damaged lung. That was over two hours ago and, except for a brief update by a nurse—*things are going as well as can be expected*—she had received no news. Until now.

"Chad," she whispered, shaking her son gently. "Chad, the doctor is coming." Chad stirred but didn't waken. Miriam whispered more urgently. "Chad! The doctor is coming. We'll find out about your father."

★ ★ ★

Pete retrieved the Jamison's car keys from the upstairs room and tossed them to Janet. "If you could run me down to the store we'll see if there's any word on Ian."

They left the Lodge and took the gravel road to where Pete had left the truck. Bess stood on the porch and watched as the big car eased into the creek and up the far bank. When she returned to the Lodge, Charlie was studying the pictures on the wall. "Over the years, we've had a number of close calls, but I can't remember going through anything like this," he said, turning to his wife.

"I can't either," she replied, linking her arm in his. "It was an awful accident, and I can't imagine what Chad is feeling right now. Do you think they're strong enough to come through this intact?"

"I really hope so. The keystone in that family is Ian, and now his life is in danger. It would be such a tragedy for them to have come so far, only to be shattered by this."

"Oh, I think Miriam and Chad are solid too. I was watching Miriam when we were awaiting word on Ian's rescue. She seemed to change." Charlie started to say something. "No, I mean it. I watched her. At first she was terrified and helpless and then...something happened! She was standing by the window in the library and...suddenly she became calm. A sense of peace just radiated from her."

★ ★ ★

The doctor approached mother and son. He was smiling. "You can go in and see him now," he said. "He's out of danger. Believe it or not, the greatest risk wasn't his lung, but the dangerous drop in his body temperature. It was a close call, but he's going to be okay."

Miriam and Chad barely heard the last part of the physician's prognosis. As soon as he had uttered the words *out of danger*, both started down the corridor to Ian's room. Opening the door, they saw a nurse adjusting an IV tube and tucking covers higher under Ian's chin. They moved quickly to his bedside.

Ian smiled groggily as his wife, and then his son, touched his arm. They were acutely aware of the injured ribs, and restrained themselves from showering him with hugs and kisses.

"How are you, Dad?" Chad said, his eyes revealing both fear and concern. "I'm so sorry you got hurt. Pete had told me about Shiloh being skittish, and I got so carried away with our trail ride, I didn't think to tell you about it!" His voice broke. "You...you were right. We should have turned back when the storm started. I'm sorry. It's just me making another stupid mistake!"

Ian raised his left arm and stroked his son's face. "Chad. Never... never say you're stupid! In fact, you were incredibly brave—and smart! You rode all the way back and got help, in spite of the storm. As for turning back, it wasn't because of the storm. I just needed an excuse! Truth be known, I wanted to go back because my backside was sore!" He started to laugh, but the pain in his chest provoked a fit of coughing.

"Don't move, Ian." Miriam began fussing over her husband, first tucking the blankets tighter around him and making sure he had water nearby. Then she fixed his pillow and placed the nurse's call-button close to his hand. "Just lay still, dear. We're so thankful you're all right. We've had a close call!"

The injured man was able to bring his discomfort under control and move to a more comfortable position. Then he signaled he wanted to speak.

"When Chad rode off to get help, I thought I wasn't going to make it. The blankets were wet, I couldn't get out of the rain, and within a few minutes I was freezing cold. I started to shiver so bad my teeth began to hurt. By the middle of the night I realized I was probably not going to see either of you again, and it made me so incredibly sad. I mean, we had just started rebuilding our lives and here I was at death's door, and it was swinging wide open to welcome me.

"I must have been going in and out of consciousness, and I began to hallucinate. There was this vision of an old man bending over me telling me to hang on, that help was on the way. I dreamed he tucked something warm around me. It was odd—it seemed so real!"

Chad was stunned! "Dad...I didn't think too much about it, but there was something weird when we got up to you with the Search and Rescue—you were fully wrapped up in one of those yellow rescue blankets! I thought maybe the medic had wrapped you in it, but now that I think about it, I was the first one to get to you."

Miriam looked at her two men and smiled. "You know what? I think there's been more going on in our lives than we realized. As you were talking about the blanket, Chad, I remembered something, not as dramatic maybe, but it's one I can't explain." She relayed how, after they had left on their trail ride, she was alone in the Lodge. She was enjoying a little time alone, sitting in the chair near the window and thumbing through a book Bess had left open on the side table. "And suddenly I had this urge to go to the bookshelf and take down a particular book. It was a volume of the sayings and writings of Kind David—a couple of thousand years ago. It fell open near the middle, and a verse just jumped out at me. It said *And the mountains shall bring peace to the people.*

"A wonderful sense of contentment and trust came over me. It was if a voice told me that things were going to be all right—regardless of how they looked on the surface. Maybe it was just coincidence, or maybe I was looking for something to hang onto, but whatever the reason, it was what I needed at that moment."

"This is really getting bizarre," Chad said, looking at his parents. "Over the past couple of weeks there have been so many strange things happening to me too. From the guy in the semi-trailer providing the police with a solid alibi, to Smudge getting in the truck, I can't count them all! And when I was riding back to get help, it was if someone was riding with me, telling me when to slow down, what rocks to watch for, and even keeping me awake in the saddle!"

★ ★ ★

A creaking sound attracted the attention of Charlie and Bess, and they hurried out the door expecting to receive word on Ian's condition.

"I think you're both right, I do believe they're keepers! The Jamisons, I mean." They were taken aback to discover a couple—even older than Bess and Charlie—sitting on the porch swing.

"Daniel! Mary! What a surprise! We weren't expecting you for a while yet!" Bess said, rushing over to hug the couple. "What are you doing here?"

"Oh, we've had a busy couple of days," Daniel said. "We were guardians for Ian and Chad during the ride but, when the storm broke and Ian was injured, we had to split up. Mary came back with Chad, and I stayed up with Ian. Quite a thunderstorm wasn't it?"

"It really was!" Charlie said. "Were you up there the whole time?"

The woman nodded. "As Daniel said, we went up to watch over Ian and Chad. I think some wonderful things have happened to that family over the last few weeks. We've been watching the transformation and we're awestruck! There was one particular incident," she looked at her husband. "I don't know if you caught it Daniel, but Ian was thanking God for bringing him and his son back together, and it was as if Chad heard his Dad. He turned in the saddle and gave him the biggest grin you've ever seen! Did you see that Daniel?"

"Of course I saw it! Did you think I was asleep?"

"No, not asleep," she kidded, "but you are getting on in years, and I thought maybe you might have dozed off for a minute or two."

"Not on your life, kiddo," he responded turning back to Bess. "You folks have done a wonderful job helping this family. To see their lives change has been a magnificent experience for us."

Bess nodded her thanks for the vote of confidence and, ever the gracious hostess, asked the guests to come inside. "Tonight's still a bit chilly from the storm. Can we tempt you with some hot chocolate?"

"If it's a package deal with some of that pie you're so famous for." Daniel replied with a hearty laugh. "We don't get down here as often as we'd like, but you know—the assignments and all?"

The group settled into the familiar chairs in front of the fireplace. "I see you haven't changed the place much have you? We had hoped to surprise you, but that old board on the porch is as squeaky as ever! Don't you ever fix things, Charlie?" Since the debacle of Charlie's poor foundation, Daniel loved teasing him.

"That board was loose when we took over from you guys Daniel," Charlie chuckled. "And we figured if you hadn't fixed it in decades, there was probably a good reason. Maybe I'll leave it for the next couple!"

Then they settled back into the warmth of the home and talked of years gone by.

Bess got up once to refresh their hot drink and bring Charlie and Daniel each a second piece of pie. She returned to her chair. "You mentioned earlier that you don't get down here as often as you like. Can I ask why you came this time? Not that we don't love having you, but I am curious."

"Actually, we have two reasons," Mary answered. "First of course, was to watch over Ian and Chad. I'm not sure we did a good job, but we're kind of limited in what we can do, other than watch over. The second was to let you folks know that God has always taken a special interest in this place—and in you—and is pleased with what's been happening. We've all been watching the families that pass through the Lodge, and the Jamison's seem to fit the bill.

"So you think these folks are the ones we've been waiting for?" Bess asked.

Daniel nodded. "We think so. Like you, we never expected the test to be so tough! But, I suppose we can never know what lies in store for any of us. All we can do is trust."

Mary continued. "I know you both are quite taken with the adult Jamisons, but I was with Chad when he rode back to get help. I'll tell you, I was impressed! He kept his wits about him and when the horse started to get winded, he resisted the impulse to keep riding hard and gave the animal a breather. Still, he kept going—even though he was cold and wet and scared. What impressed me the most was his determination. He had made a commitment and he followed through."

"It was touch and go there for a while—for both of them. Ian's injury was nasty, and Chad's riding all night through the rain and darkness on a horse he didn't know was pretty risky."

"Wasn't there any way you folks could have helped?"

Daniel grinned. "Who said we didn't?"

EPILOGUE

SCATTERED CLOUDS ABOVE THE LAKE DRIFTED OFF IN the early afternoon, chased by a gentle breeze that eased them westward and over the horizon. A bald eagle, wings catching the upper edge of a draft, soared above an old hunting lodge set on the crest of a hill overlooking the water.

Emerging from the trees, a slow moving figure made his way down a path leading to the front porch. He ambled along, enjoying the late-summer rays that filtered through the leaves and laid a dappled pattern on the dusty surface. He was a middle-aged man, probably in his mid-fifties, taking his time and soaking up nature's sensations as he walked along. He heard the whisper of the breeze through the trees, the cry of the eagle circling high overhead, and the sound of lake water lapping the shore below the lodge. As the warmth of the sun filtered through the foliage and touched his face, he paused a moment to watch a squirrel scamper up a nearby tree.

Life for this man had recently taken unexpected turns. In his plans he had never listed *lodge keeper* as a goal. But he and his wife had been asked, and instinctively agreed. As he climbed the steps onto the porch, he looked out over the placid lake, paused for a moment, and gave thanks for what life had brought them.

"How are things in town?" the woman asked as she opened the door. She carried a glass of cold lemonade in her right hand and offered it to him.

"Great!" he replied. "You know that inquiry we made with that ranch? You know, the one we visited earlier this year?" He nodded his thanks for the cool beverage.

His wife answered with excitement. "Yes I do remember them! Are they going to come up for a visit?"

"Well, I'm not too sure why they're coming up, but it looks like they'll be here tomorrow afternoon."

"Did you remember to put up the sign at the corner? We don't want our guests getting lost coming up here."

The man shook his head. "No, not yet. They won't be arriving until later tomorrow, so maybe the two of us can walk down and put it up in the morning?" The woman nodded.

"Did you tell them to bring the sign up with them when they came?" she asked. She knew the routine for new arrivals.

He nodded. "Yes I did. Do you remember the first time we came up here? We almost forgot to take it down? I wonder what would have happened if we hadn't removed it?"

She became thoughtful. "We'll never know. But I do know that no one had ever arrived here without bringing it. From what Bess told me, that tradition began many years ago, and was established as a result of someone trying to contact his ex-girlfriend who was staying up here with her family." She stood, about to re-enter the house. "I want to show you something," she said, taking hold of her husband's arm. He rose and joined her.

Arm in arm, they entered the main room of the Lodge. "I was looking at these pictures earlier," she said, pointing at the photos. "There are so many hurts in those families, and those hurts all involve conflict. Conflict with parents, with spouses, with siblings and, sometimes, even conflict with themselves.

"While the families all had their own particular hurts to work through, and we have seen miracles happen, I believe there was a common factor in each of those healing processes.

"These are all pictures of the families who came up here, along with the individual who sent them." He looked more closely at them. "That's a picture of Mrs. Tarkowski standing with Janet and her Mom."

Looking at another one, the man commented, "And that's Sergeant Kostiak with the MacDonald family. And here's a picture of the Thatcher's and their daughters, with Ginny Bellows, the social worker."

"And look at this one," his wife instructed. "It's my favorite!"

Ian chucked. "That's my favorite as well. Just you, Chad and I standing with Judge Stevenson. But what are you getting at? What was it that everyone shared?"

"I'm talking about the one thing that was common in the healing of each family. And I don't mean good food, warm beds or wonderful conversation. Those, without a doubt, were crucial to the healing, but there was more. In each instance, the healing involved horses. Sometimes, such as with our family, it was a trip up into the mountains on the horses. With others, as was the case with the MacDonalds, it was working with one particular horse. Even going back all the way with Pete and Janet, it was horses that brought them together."

★ ★ ★

It was late morning when the couple began their walk from the Lodge to where the dusty lane intersected the main road. They recalled the first time they had driven down this lane toward the Lodge. They reflected on their uncertainty, even fear, of what awaited them.

Relying solely on a hand-drawn map, they had put their trust, hope and faith in the integrity and advice of another. They recalled the months prior to their appearance in the courtroom and the feelings of helplessness and foreboding.

Their thoughts and conversation wandered back over the years since their first arrival at Lake Sandoza. Chad was now in his final year of university and was pursuing a career in geology. Pete and Janet were still wranglers at the Lodge, and they now had two children of their own—a four-year old daughter and a brand new baby boy, born just this past spring.

Charlie and Bess came around once in a while. The old couple's tasks and assignments had taken new directions, but their love of the Lodge and its people remained strong.

Miriam took the sign Ian was carrying and, together, they placed it carefully and lovingly in its posthole alongside the road. The new *Keepers of the Lodge* headed back down the lane to anxiously await the new arrivals.

But these arrivals promised to be both very different and very interesting.

An exciting time lay ahead.

ACKNOWLEDGEMENTS

THE DIFFICULTY WITH COMPILING A LIST OF PEOPLE who were instrumental in the writing and publication of *any* book, is that there are so many. This is not a work that started on a specific date and concluded on another. It is a journey—a journey that began when I was very young, a journey that continues.

I have been singularly blessed by the men and women who disciplined, mentored, taught and influenced me throughout my life. Chief among those were my parents, Gordon and Margaret MacInnes, whose lives were shining examples of the *foundation cornerstones* described in this book.

To the incredible people at the Anasazi Foundation. The work they do with youth and families has a positive effect on people and programs around the world. I have witnessed the gentling of hearts at war, the reuniting of families and the transforming of lives.

This is the second edition of this book, and it was Jeremy Drought, who steered this project through many challenges, always under the pressure of deadlines, and always with quiet class and professionalism.

Wayne Magnuson, whose skillful use of the editor's scalpel made this a far better book than was originally drafted, I give my gratitude and appreciation. His thoughtful comments and questions pushed me to be a better writer. The plot became cleaner, the setting more real, the dialogue more precise, and the learning moments more refined.

To Friesen Publishing, I express my thanks for believing in the project, reading and refining the manuscript, and bringing forward a finished book that we are all proud of.

However, it is to my wife, Dee, who deserves my greatest thanks. It was she who listened to endless hours of rambling, who read repeated drafts, who provided insights and ideas that informed many of the scenes and conversations in this book. I often wondered why the characters spoke to her, while giving me the silent treatment! She just has that way with people. I love you.

Ross A. MacInnes

CONTACT THE AUTHOR

The author is available for workshops and clinics or for keynote addresses at various events and functions. To contact Ross or to gain additional insight into his background and experience, please go to

www.rossamacinnes.com

Read on for an excerpt from Ross MacInnes's book

CHAPTER ONE

I must be getting old. I had laid down during the night and the damp ground had brought on another touch of arthritis. Now, ambling down the path, I glanced back and saw Toto and some of the other older horses who had also spent the night amongst the trees in the upper pasture. The people around the ranch called us "the war vets," as we had been around the place for many years working cattle drives, riding fences, pulling logs and finding lost calves. As our paces slowed and our turns became stiffer, we were gradually relieved of our duties and allowed to graze quietly, sleep later and enjoy our retirement. Oh, from time to time friends of The Man would come out to the ranch and kids would climb on our backs and we'd walk around the pasture carrying them. As long as we got some carrots and a good brushing, it was kind of a good life for us.

As more and more of us were getting on in years, heading up the hill to the security and calmness of the trees was becoming a routine. But I wanted to check on the rest of the herd, so turned and continued the journey down the winding trail to the open meadow near the barn. On the way, I passed Legend and Pita still holding their positions from standing watch over the herd during the dark hours. Pita was a big fellow. I had learned from The Man that this horse was part Percheron and part Thoroughbred. His recent past was one of running wild in a nearby forest reserve with a herd of wild mustangs. Humans had tried to tame him, but he always threw them off his back—he enjoyed running free too much to be put in a small paddock or be paraded around in some arena. After breaking a trainer's leg at a nearby ranch by throwing him off, he was given the name Pita. I learned it stood for Pain in the Ass—not a very nice name to call that tall black horse. But after coming here he, like the rest of us, felt comfortable enough to let humans ride on us.

Legend was fairly new to the herd, but made a big impact when he arrived. It sounds odd to say it (even to me), but he was bigger than Pita. He was even bigger than the Clydesdales. But he had a very gentle way about him. Like Pita, he was solid black with not even one white hair. While The Man enjoyed being with all of us, he did take a bit of extra pride in Legend. I overheard him being described as a "Canadian Horse—one of only a few left in the world." I wanted to be jealous of him, but he was so gentle I couldn't dislike him. Not like some of the other horses who have come here over the years!

The stronger mares and geldings—usually those in their mature years—always stood guard to protect the herd from prowling cougars, wolves or other predators. As horses, we can see exceptionally well at night and, by taking a position upwind of the sleeping herd, we can also scent danger from a long distance. And by locking our front legs, we can stand for many hours without moving. But it's a tough job, always being on the alert for threats. However, it gives the rest of the herd comfort in that they can feel safe.

I feel sorry for horses who aren't in a herd. They don't really get good rests, and never really feel safe. I wish humans could understand us better. We need a herd, and we need leaders for the herd.

I gave each a nod as I left the trees. Both Legend and Pita would wait until most of the horses were up and moving, take a drink of water, have some grazing time then snooze for most of the day.

The colts were racing around, kicking up a storm. Rearing up at each other then, quick as could be, dropping down and trying to bite the opponent's leg. The object was to force the other horse to lift his one front leg, become unbalanced and, with a quick dive, the opposing colt would bump the off-balanced horse and bring him to the ground.

It didn't always work, but they would play the game for what seemed like hours. Once in a while one would break off and race away with the other chasing.

It was a game I played often as a colt, and still played, although not as often or as athletically as I once did. The years of riding deep into the mountains, hauling supplies up to remote camps and herding cattle at round-ups had taken its toll. My back is a constant bother, my knees complain, particularly on damp or chilly days, and even my eyesight isn't what it once was. But I can still hold my own with the younger horses. What I now lack in skill and speed, I more than make up for with wisdom and experience.

As the trail exited the upper pasture into the paddock surrounding the barn I stopped a moment to quietly absorb my surroundings. The barn formed the center of the yard, with hay sheds, tractor garage, storage shacks and an old chicken coop fanning out from that point. The buildings weren't enclosed by fences, and it was always a help in blustery weather to be able to huddle out of the wind on the lee side of the buildings. It was quite a change from the previous ranch where I had been raised. At that place, everything was fenced off and we were never allowed to walk through the alleys beside the structures. Here, at the Triple R Ranch, only the visitor's cars were fenced off—the remaining area was open to the horses. And, if the visitors didn't bother putting their cars in the car corral, it was fair game for the colts and fillies to lick the paint, chew the wipers or mug themselves in the mirrors, which they often did.

The lower pasture dropped off to the north, bordered by a row of poplar trees atop a deep coulee. To the east the fence marked the end of our property and the beginning of hundreds of acres of barley. At this time of year it was all stubble, and Old Man Jespersen had let his cattle in to pick among the stalks, searching out those few elusive kernels that had escaped the combine and fallen to the ground.

And to the west, the miles of prairie grass, marred only by Highway 112, continued on to the base of the distant mountains.

Coming off the trail and into the main yard near the barn, I saw that most of the horses were now up and moving around. The early morning sun highlighted the tops of the fence posts and, while the distant foothills were still in shadows, the sunlit tops of the Rocky Mountains promised a warm autumn day ahead.

Now this may seem to be a strange way to start a discussion, but you'll just have to bear with me as I try to explain a few things.

This whole process began as a result of a random musing by the human I call "The Man." There were other humans at the Triple R— the foreman called "Cinch," a lady that was often with The Man and a number of regular people who came to the ranch and worked with the horses. They also did some of the work around the place. But The Man had been around the ranch longer than me and, in fact, was the one who first brought me here and was the first human I learned to trust. He always spoke quietly, never seemed bothered by anything, had a gentle and light hand when he rode and always took time to talk with me. He was taller than most humans and walked with a bit of a limp, but was always able to mount smoothly into the saddle. I had never seen him without his battered old hat pulled low over his forehead, and I had never seen him without a smile. I kind of think he enjoyed being with us.

On this particular morning, I watched as he walked down into the pasture. Sometimes he just comes to the gate and calls a particular horse, but this time he came into the field where we were grazing. He approached and slipped a halter over my head—I thought we were going out for a ride or something. As he was buckling the throatlatch, he looked over and saw our herd leader, Tucker, gently pushing one of the horses up the hill.

You see, one of the "war vets," a twenty-nine-year-old Quarterhorse, had gotten himself cut on a tree branch, and was having difficulty walking up to the barn. Tucker was doing what he always did—making sure every horse in the herd was taken care of.

Old Squirrel (yes, that's what they called him!) had a great career as a roping horse, but had been retired here at the ranch for about ten years. The kids loved him and he was one of the favorites. But his coordination wasn't what it once was, and I guess in going up the path through the bush, he had stumbled and cut himself quite badly on the branch.

Anyway, when The Man stopped tugging on me and was bright enough to follow along, I took him over to where Tucker and Squirrel were standing. I thought he should be aware of Squirrel's cut and take him into the barn to treat the wound.

He stood there for a few minutes, just observing. Tucker looked at The Man, and then went back to his task of helping Squirrel up the hill to the barn.

We watched as the elderly horse struggled to keep his feet and move along the path. When Squirrel would tire, Tucker would pause long enough for the elderly horse to catch his breath, then gently push him forward toward the main doors.

The thirty-eight other horses in the herd politely stood back, letting Tucker do his work. On one occasion a young gelding moved a bit too close but, when Tucker pinned his ears and gave a quick look at the offender, the youngster quickly moved back to a respectable distance.

We followed along, not interfering, just keeping a respectful distance and letting Tucker do his work. It was becoming apparent that The Man was fascinated by the unfolding scene. That's when he made his comment: "Caddie, I'd sure like to know how this whole 'herd leadership' thing works."

And that got me thinking that maybe I should pass on what I've learned over the years. Which horse gets to be the herd leader, its characteristics and, maybe just as important—why the rest of the herd will follow.

★ ★ ★

When I first came to the ranch there were only six horses. Now, with forty horses, the dynamics of the herd had changed dramatically.

Back then, the unquestioned leader of our small herd was a Thoroughbred named Murphy.

On arrival, Murphy soon made his presence felt. Not content with the size of the holding corral, he figured out that a couple of good pushes would open the slide gate and give him full access to acres and acres of lush grass in the lower pasture. When we look back at every mischievous horse event we can see Murphy's hoofprints somewhere in the background.

You see, Murphy had an injury on the track. During one particular race, he "bowed" his right tendon. For most horses this was a career-ending injury, and it should have been for Murphy as well. But his owners thought they might be able to squeeze just one more season out of him, and so had a painful and highly questionable procedure done. It's called "pinfiring."

Now, I may be a bit biased being a horse and all, but to my thinking, this was a barbaric and painful practice. It involved the insertion of hot pins into the front of the shin. The belief was that it sped up healing, although many veterinarians disagree with the concept and with the supposed benefits. That process has been forbidden now for many years, but back in Murphy's day it was actually quite common.

What did occur was that Murphy became very wary and afraid of people, particularly when they tried to examine the affected leg. Murphy had both his forelegs done in this manner. And even after enduring this practice he never had an extension to his racing career. He was extremely anti-social and would throw himself over backwards rather than allow a human on his back. When tied he would rip the post from its mountings and race through the field pulling a hitching rail behind.

But through patience, love and gentle handling from the humans here at Triple R, Murphy became leader of the herd.

As you may have gathered by now, we began as a small herd—just a few of us. We came to the ranch with lots of problems, but The Man and the rest of the humans here really seemed to take our fears and hurts personally. They always tried their best to help us along.

Murphy was The Man's special horse. I often watched as Murphy would lay his ears back flat along his head and try to toss The Man off his back and onto the ground. In fact, I think he wanted to really hurt The Man if he could. But as time went on and the two of them spent time together, they developed a special relationship. I wanted to trust The Man, but I had been disappointed too many times to just put my trust in *any* human. But the care he gave Murphy and the patient way he let that coal-black Thoroughbred show his anger and frustration yet still never beat him or hurt him in any way, gave me hope that, over time, I too could trust this human.

Tucker hadn't come to the ranch yet—it was just Murphy, four other geldings and me. We had lots of attention from The Man in those early years. He spent time with each of us, although I admit that sometimes I was envious of the special friendship he had with Murphy. But when The Man would come down to the pasture to bring one of us up to go for a ride, we all trotted to the gate to meet him. He usually had a carrot or other treat with him, and would spend time just being with us. I always wanted him to take me to go riding with, but he mostly took Murphy.

Over the years, he and Murphy did a lot of riding. I do know that retired racehorse got more attention than any of us, but he also worked his heart out for The Man. One of their regular outings was the trip up to the line camp. They didn't go up there very often—usually during calving season in the spring, or to overnight during the fall roundup. But I know from the excitement both showed that it was a favorite time for them.

I heard The Man once telling a friend of his that there was a special feeling when coming around the last bend in the trail and seeing that old shack come into view. It was kind of tucked back into a hill, the old front porch sagging from the many cowboys lounging on it after working cattle all day. The steps down from the deck were well worn, and the hitching rail had seen many years of use. There was a tin-pipe chimney sticking out of the roof, and a couple hooks tucked up beneath the overhang where The Man would hang his coat before going inside the shack. And just over from the steps was a small corral with a shelter for the horses of the cowboys who either spent weeks up there throughout calving, or stayed for the short term during the fall roundup. A lot of work got done there, but it was also a place of solitude and peace.

As the elder statesman of the herd, Murphy packed supplies up to line camp and did dozens of little duties, such as dallying a reluctant newcomer horse across the creek, or hauling water up to the north pastures. For a gelding once considered a top race contender, these jobs might have seemed mundane, but for Murphy, they were labors of love. And as the herd grew, so did Murphy's responsibilities. In spite of his early behavior, he became the standard for all leaders to come.

But, as Murphy became older, injuries from his past began to affect him and he could no longer carry the weight of The Man. But he still loved to go on rides anytime he could. I remember the first time I went up to the line camp with The Man while he let his favorite horse walk alongside. No halter, bridle, saddle or anything. And Murphy just tagged along.

As we came up the trail toward the camp, Murphy moved ahead of us, trotted around the corner and disappeared. When we arrived at the steps, there was that old horse just waiting for us. He tossed his head as if to question our delay, and whinnied until The Man opened the corral gate, let both Murphy and I in, and gave us a measure of oats. The horses always got a bit of oats after making the trip from the main ranch up to line camp.

You see, when The Man asked me about herd leadership, I had to start at the beginning of my education. Over the years I have watched and learned about leadership and the characteristics displayed by horses that rise to lead.

Murphy led the herd for a number of years—through storms, additions to the herd, new pastures, corrals, and yes, even through the departing of some great stallions, mares and geldings as they completed their journey. His was truly the first real demonstration of herd leadership I had experienced.

But my learning was just beginning. It's time you got to know Tucker.

CPSIA information can be obtained
at www.ICGtesting.com
Printed in the USA
LVOW11s1248220317
528072LV00002B/18/P